Chindi Authors Present

A Feast of Christmas Stories:

Unwrap a Sussex Tale

A Chindi Production

Cover photograph and artwork by Helen Christmas

Editors: Patricia Feinberg Stoner, Julia Macfarlane,
Rosemary Noble and Angela Petch.

©   The First Christmas of the War by Beryl Kingston
©   Tiny Tim by Christopher Joyce
©   Side by Side by Alan Readman
©   The Christmas Present by Maralyn Green
©   Moonshadows by Bruce Macfarlane
©   Christmas Spirit by Carol Thomas
©   The Knucker's First Christmas by Patricia
       Feinberg Stoner
©   Pudding by Lexi Rees
©   Christmas Repeats by Phil Clinker
©   Stranger on the Shore by Angela Petch
©   The Best-Behaved Girl in Bognor by Julia
       Macfarlane
©   Winter Solstice by Patricia Osborne
©   Chilblains by Isabella Muir
©   The Gift by Susanne Heywood
©   When the Bee Choir Sings by Rosemary Noble
©   The Mystery of the Phantom Santa by Peter
       Bartram

© 2019 Chindi Authors

Chichester Publishing

ISBN 9 781999 864453

"I wouldn't mind that for my Christmas present," he says.

"Would they buy it for you?" His Mum and Dad are my aunt and uncle and they're not stingy so I'll bet they would.

"I expect so," he says. "If I asked them to."

I wish I could ask Mum to buy me the theatre. She wouldn't, of course, because it's so much money. Five whole pounds. It's a fortune. Two and a half times as much as Daddy earns in a week. I know what he earns because Gran told me once.

"Couldn't you have some games with that theatre," I say. "I wouldn't mind that for my Christmas present."

Alan's working out how long it would take him to save up enough money to buy a box of soldiers. "Eight half crowns in a pound," he says. "That's eight weeks."

"You'd have to go without sweets," I tell him. He buys sweets every week. He loves sweets. He's storing them for when they go on ration. Only he keeps eating the store and then he has to buy more.

"Um," he says, considering it. "Eight weeks is a long time."

I'm still lusting after the theatre. "How long would it take to save up for the toy theatre?"

We stand in front of the window, gazing at our inaccessible dreams, doing mental arithmetic. "Eight weeks a pound, five times eight is forty, forty weeks."

"Forty weeks," I say. "That's ten months." We both know it's impossible and we both say so. But wouldn't it be wonderful.

"Come on," he says. "Better be getting back or it'll be dark."

So we leave the dazzle of the toyshop and go home through the darkening footpath where the rooks caw and jump into the air and the brambles claw at us as we pass.

But I can't leave the theatre behind. I dream of it every night. I'm writing plays for it and arranging the little characters and switching on the lights and opening the red velvet curtains to reveal it in all its glory.

"Happy Christmas!" the teachers call to us as we leave on the last day of term. "You've earned it, all of you. You've been wonderful. Happy Christmas." I wonder whether it will be. You never know in my house.

Dad's coming down for Christmas, so Mum says. She says he couldn't come before because his firm has been evacuated to Hertfordshire and it's too far. I wonder whether he'll bring us any presents. Alan's got his from his mum and dad. Aunty Ela brought it down for him, because it's only a few days till Christmas now and she won't be able to get down again because of the shop. She and Uncle Leslie run an Off Licence and Christmas is the busiest time of the year. Alan says he doesn't mind. And Gran says. "Don't worry about him, Ela. He'll be all right with us."

So now it's just a matter of waiting the last few days. We have fires in the bungalow now because it's getting very cold and in the evening we all sit round and listen to the wireless. Our favourite programme is Tommy Handley's ITMA, which is short for 'It's That Man Again.' It's ever so funny and ever so quick and it makes us laugh like anything. Mum says it's an absolute tonic. Tommy Handley's really good. He pokes fun at everything and says the most amazing things and he gives all the characters peculiar names. There's a charlady called Mrs Tickle who says 'I always does my best for all my gentlemen,' and a man called Fusspot, who makes a fuss about everything, and another one called Vodkin who speaks in a funny accent and calls Tommy Handley all sorts of funny names like Mr Handmedown and Mr Hamaneggs, and a man who phones up and pretends to be Hitler and says, 'This is Fumf speaking.' The door keeps opening all through the programme and you never know what's going to come in next. It could be a person or a tank or a flock of sheep or anything. I love it. There's going to be a special show for Christmas, and I can't wait for it.

We couldn't get a turkey this year, but Gran's got two chickens and she's made an enormous Christmas pudding. It was steaming in the kitchen for hours and hours and the whole place smells of it. She says it'll make very good eating.

It does too. Alan licks his plate and they don't tell him off, and Dad says it's the best meal he's had since he was evacuated, and nobody's cross. I think this is going to be the best Christmas ever.

After dinner we make up the fire, clear the plates and leave them in the sink to soak, shake the cloth out in the garden and put the chenille cloth on the table, and then we all gather round the fire for the presents, which have been waiting on the sofa bed for days and days, looking tempting.

Dad gives Mum his present first. It's a pair of silk stockings and she says, 'Very nice' and actually thanks him. That's a good start because she usually just sniffs when he gives her a present. Then Gran gives him some of his

9

favourite tobacco, and Alan gets his lead soldiers, which is nice, and me and Alan give Gran some Yardley's lavender water, which is her favourite, and I get a Rupert Annual and a Pinocchio colouring-in book and a new packet of colouring pencils. I always get the Rupert Bear annual and I always say it's very nice and thank you very much because that's what they expect, but I don't really like it. Rupert Bear's a goody-goody and the book's boring. But the colouring pencils are nice.

The last two presents are one to Mum from Gran and one to my sister, labelled 'Dear little Pat, from her Mummy and Daddy.' Mum reads it out before she gives it to her. It's a very big present, all done up in brown paper, and it takes her a long time to unwrap it, while we all watch and tell her to hurry up and to come on, which is what you have to do.

But she opens it at last and takes it out of its box and it's my toy theatre. It's such a shock I feel as if someone's punched me in the stomach. My lovely theatre! Given to her! It's awful. Whatever made them give her an expensive present like that? She'll ruin it! She's much too young for it. It says suitable for children aged ten to fourteen on the side of the box - I can see it from where I'm sitting - and she's only just four. Much, much too young. She won't know how to play with it. She doesn't know anything about theatres. And I do. It's not fair. Not, not, not. How could they do such a thing? If they wanted to give it to anyone they should have given it to me. I'm the right age for it and I could have played with it beautifully. Now I've got to watch while she scribbles on it and tears it to bits and throws it about. She won't let me have a go of it because she'll say it's hers. I don't think I can bear it.

She's picking up the little characters by their heads. Oh don't do that. Treat them gently. They're delicate. "What is it?" she says, looking puzzled.

"It's a theatre, darling," Mum says. "Won't that be a lovely thing to play with."

Christmas is over and it's been snowing for days and days. The whole world's white and black, as if someone's come along during the night and rubbed out all the colour. The roofs are all quite white and so are the pavements and the fences, and the beach is under a foot of snow. People go out with spades and shovels and clear their front paths and as much of the pavement as they can, but you can't see where the gardens begin and end, and the branches of the trees are twice the size because they're coated in ice.

Mum has fires halfway up the chimney, but they only warm the living room and the rest of the bungalow is freezing. When you wake up in the morning you can see your breath streaming out in front of you, as if you're out of doors, and we keep our socks on in bed because the lino strikes so cold when you get up. Me and Alan get dressed under the covers too so as to keep warm. When I'm grown-up I'm going to have carpets and fires in every room in my house. The windows are so cold it hurts to touch them and they're covered in swirling patterns of ice. They start in the corners right at the bottom and grow upwards until they cover half the windowpane, and they're actually rather pretty, like fern leaves and flowers. Most mornings, me and Alan lift up the net curtains to have a look at them, but we don't look long because the cold air puffs in through the cracks round the window and makes us shiver. Even with two jerseys on and two pairs of socks you still feel cold. And I've got chilblains.

When I first had them, I didn't know what they were. My toes felt as though they were on fire and when I took my socks off they were all swollen up like bright red sausages. So I showed them to Gran and she said "Chilblains. I'll get you some Wintergreen." It's a stick of ointment that you have to rub on. It stings like anything, but it does take the burning away. The only trouble is that afterwards your toes start itching and you can't scratch through your shoes and socks, especially when you're walking to school.

It takes us a long time to get through the snow to school because you have to trudge. We wear wellington boots because the drifts come halfway up our legs, and winter coats and woolly hats and scarves and gloves, but when the wind blows it can cut through anything. Your hands get so cold your fingers go white. You have to suck them to warm them up or put them under your armpits and, when you do that, you can feel the cold leaking out into your chest. I don't think they ought to make you go to school when it's as cold as this. You ought to be allowed to stay at home and sit by the fire all day like Pat. But no, they bundle you up and send you out no matter what. Even when the sea freezes.

It was frozen yesterday morning. There were great sheets of solid ice at the water's edge and the tide was pushing them forward and clunking them against each other. The sea is dark grey now like the tree trunks and the bits of the main road that they've cleared with snow ploughs or melted with grit. I've almost forgotten what it

12

looks like when it's green. It says in the paper that it's the worst winter for fifty years. The Thames has frozen over too and that's the first time since 1888. I wish it would hurry up and go away. I'd really like to feel warm again.

Mum's been in a bad mood since Christmas. They've started the rationing and she can't buy enough butter and bacon and sugar. Gran's really upset because she loves butter and spreads it on her bread in great thick slices. You can buy as much marg as you want but she doesn't like marg. She says it tastes like axle grease and she wouldn't eat it if you paid her. Mum says she doesn't know what the government's playing at. It isn't as if there's really a war on, not when all's said and done. But our teacher says we're being rationed because the U-boats have been sinking our supply ships and rationing is the only way to see that we all get fair shares. Which makes sense.

Actually, I don't think it's just the rationing that's making Mum so touchy. She gets cross at the least little thing and she's watching me all the time. Sometimes I feel as though she's willing me to be naughty. Although that can't be right because she wants me to be good. That's why she canes me. She's always saying so. She says I would be hateful if it wasn't for that cane. I'd quite like to be hateful sometimes. It's three weeks now since Christmas and Pat's ruined the theatre. Every time we come home from school, she's broken a bit more of it. She's scribbled all over the proscenium arch and pulled the heads off the characters and broken the lights and snapped all the little poles in half and now it's standing on the dresser all battered and in bits. It makes me ache to look at it, and I mustn't say anything.

13

I did once and it was horrible. I asked her to let me have a go of it. I shouldn't have, and it made me feel really awful to ask, as if they were hitting me, but I did so want to play with it and it wouldn't have hurt her. I could have shown her what to do. It didn't get me anywhere. She yelled out for Mum at once, "Mummy! Mummy! Beryl's taking my toys!" And Mum came in and said I was to leave her alone or I'd get the cane. "It's her theatre," she said. "You play with your own toys and stop being so jealous."

So now I just read my library books and trudge into Bognor once a week to change them. I do wish this war could be over and it could be Spring again. Gran says we've got to make the best of things, so I suppose that's what we've got to do, but I can't see much good in snow and freezing cold. The books are good though. I've found some lovely ones. Some by E Nesbit that I hadn't read and lots of fairy stories and a whole set about a boy called William who is always getting into trouble. I like him very much, especially as he has to put up with a horrible little spoilt brat called Violet Elizabeth Bott. Somebody should whack her! I wonder whether they will in the next book. I hate spoilt brats, especially when people give them expensive presents and they pull them to bits. They should be taken out in the garden with no coat on and buried under the snow. Now that would be good.

Beryl Kingston

Beryl Kingston is a prolific author of plays, short stories, occasional poetry and 30 novels in various genres: 26 published with number 27 called 'Citizen Armies' due for publication in September 2019 by Endeavour Media.

'I started writing a diary when I was seven,' she says, 'which is 82 years ago, and kept it all through the war. Very useful.

'I write every day. My first book was published in 1980, when I was 49, and was called 'Lifting the Curse'. My first novel came out in 1985 and was called 'Hearts and Farthings'. My sales passed the million mark with book 12. I have never suffered from writer's block.

'I am currently working on book 31, which is called 'That damned old woman' and features a totally dishonest politician who has told so many lies he can't recognise the truth.'

Tiny Tim and the Glittery Reindeer
by Christopher Joyce

December 22nd

I don't believe it! It's Tiny Tim again. That's the third day in a row he's wandered around the Christmas display with his sticky little fingers touching everything. I bet his parents drop him off then go and have a burger and a couple of pints of lager.

"Hey, mister, what's the reindeer called?"

"Windy."

The chubby little kid with the ridiculous Christmas-pudding-shaped bobble hat reached out to touch the centrepiece of my display with a puzzled look.

"Is that because he flies as fast as the wind?"

"No, it's because he's eaten all the Brussels sprouts." The little munchkin has no idea what I'm talking about, so I squeeze my nose and wave my hand behind my bum. He looks horrified then screws up his squidgy little face.

"I don't like sprouts."

"And I don't like sticky fingers," I say, rearranging some donkeys that bray when you lift their tails and dispense chestnuts. You can guess where from.

In the seven years I've worked at the Chichester Garden Centre, this has to be the most bizarre selection of gifts ever. I mean, who wants to buy a snow globe with Darth Vader, two penguins and something that was supposed to be a small puppy, but looks more like a pile of poop with eyes?

Tiny Tim is still staring at Windy.

"I like his shiny antlers," he says, wiping his nose on the sleeve of his "Ho Ho Ho it's Christmas" jumper.

The kid's dead if he knocks over my display. It took me weeks to arrange the dancing dolls from *Frozen* with the Disney "lifelike" Christmas trees with musical baubles. Each plastic globe holds a highly detailed figurine that comes with its own theme tune. If I turn the lot on at once, it looks like a Disneyland office party on class A drugs.

Tiny Tim wobbles over to the selection of yuletide logs filled with chocolate liqueurs. I point a customer in the direction of the door wreaths and turn back expecting to find half a dozen empty chocolate wrappers, but the logs are all intact.

December 23rd

I thought for a moment my little friend might not show today, but here he is again with a lovely new hat that looks like a giant mince pie, and yet another Christmas jumper with "Elf and Safety" written on it. Jeez, his parents really know how to spoil this kid.

"Do Windy's antlers light up?" he asks, picking up a festive fountain that drowns three little angels in plastic snow.

"Only if you pour a can of petrol on them," I reply, feeling a little mean to the poor guy. "Where are your parents? Are they shopping for plants?"

17

He shrugs, and I begin to fear that they really have dropped him off then gone to the bookies or something.

"Do you know the names of the elves that make all the presents?" he asks me, rubbing his piggy little eyes with his woollen mitten.

"Not unless they're called Wu Ping." Most of the tat we sell is made in China. I wonder what Wu and his mates think Christmas is all about? Probably means extra shifts and sleeping under your workstation until you've covered a thousand plastic antlers with white paint and glitter.

My colleague tells me the store manager wants to see me. That means I'm in trouble again. I leave Tiny Tim playing with the wind-up cherubs and knock on her door.

"Come," says a voice that's had enough of tinsel and crackers. "Yes, I'm on it like a fat kid on a hot dog," she says and hangs up. There's a poster behind her desk of Cliff Richard promoting his *Best Christmas Songs Ever* with several darts piercing his left cheek.

"Nice grouping," I say, hoping to get a wee smile to creep across Sallie's face, but she's not exactly full of Christmas spirit, although there is an empty whisky bottle poking out from the Excel spreadsheets in the bin to the side of her desk.

December 24th

Got away with it yesterday, just. Apparently, someone had complained that I'd upset their little girl by wearing my "Santa is dead" T-shirt. I had thought I was in trouble for telling her sister the elves had all come down with food poisoning, so there would be no toys this Christmas.

It's been a long day as some idiot decided it would be good to stay open until 9 p.m. on Christmas Eve. We're closing in twenty minutes, and I think Tiny Tim is a no-show until a rotund ball of red and gold comes into sight.

"Hey, kid, haven't you got a home to go to?"

He puts down the glow-in-the-dark snowman and takes off his white igloo-shaped bobble hat to scratch his bald head. There are a few wisps of hair and an angry-looking scar above his left ear. I take a step back and knock over the dancing dolls.

"It's okay, mister. It doesn't hurt. Mummy says the drug stuff will take the tumour away."

I'm lost for words, but he's calm and smiling at me. "Here, have a chocolate penguin," he says and helps me pick up the dolls that are trying to escape to the safety of the Christmas cactus display. I chase some down that have wedged themselves under the display cabinet and then I crawl out. The little bugger's wandered off before I could ask him why he's here.

I take a swig from the bottle of port hidden in my desk and ask Rosemary at the front desk if she's seen the little fat kid.

"Oh, you mean Tim Cratchit. Yes, his parents bring him here after his chemo at the hospital. Lovely lad; put on a lot of weight since he started the treatment though."

She writes down their address from the loyalty-scheme database. I grab Windy and bung him in the back of my car with his two hind legs hanging out the passenger window. Ten minutes later I'm at a neat little council house with a large wreath on the door. I ring the doorbell. A young girl answers.

"Is your dad in? I've got a present for Tim."

Her father appears at the door a little taken aback by the sight of a man holding a six-foot reindeer.

"That's very kind of you, but I'm afraid Tim's been in hospital for a few weeks. He's been under heavy sedation for the last five days. He's a fighter; he'll be fine."

I stare at him as if I've just seen three wise men pull up in Santa's sleigh.

"You're the guy from the garden centre aren't you? Tim says you always make him laugh. I'm Bob. This is my daughter Martha." He holds out a hand and smiles.

I take his hand, still trying to make sense of the last few days.

"Eddie," I mumble. "Eddie Neaser."

Martha takes my other hand, and they insist I come in for a glass of sherry and a mince pie.

"My wife is at the hospital," Bob explains. "We take it in turns. They're amazing up at St Richard's. Angels really – every one of them."

Martha hands me a warm mince pie, which I decline. "I'm sorry, but there's something I need to do tonight, and it can't wait."

They look puzzled as I rush out of the house, leaving Windy on the doorstep. A group of carol singers is outside the neighbour's house. I put a fifty-pound note in the collection box. The choirmaster is stunned; she stares at the crumpled note. "God bless us every one," she says to the back of my head as I climb into my car.

The drive back to the garden centre and then on to the cathedral takes a few minutes, and to be honest, it's all a bit of a blur. I park down a side street with a sign that warns "permit holders only", but I need to get to the cathedral before it fills up with the devoted and deliriously drunk for midnight mass.

The choir is rehearsing and "Hark! the Herald Angels Sing" booms out of the massive organ. The smell of freshly lit candles fills the air, and I dodge a few officials handing out leaflets to make my way to the children's crib positioned by the font.

All the usual players have gathered. There is Mary in her blue robe looking surprisingly calm considering she gave birth a few hours ago, and now she's surrounded by sheep, cows and some dodgy-looking foreigners.

I dig into my pocket and find the plastic figure stolen from "Santa's glow-in-the-dark Lapland workshop". The reindeer doesn't have glittery antlers, but at least he has a shiny red nose. I pocket the cow nearest to baby Jesus and replace her with Rudolph.

"This is for Tim, Wu and all the other kids that can't be home for Christmas," I say to a small angel hovering over the stall.

Christopher Joyce

Christopher Joyce lives in central Chichester. The city has inspired his series of children's books *The Creatures of Chichester* available as e-books, audio books and printed books designed to be dyslexic friendly. His stories feature popular pets and smaller animals that work together to solve the problems created by the Twolegs (or humans).

He has also produced The Alien Cookbook for kids of all ages featuring Gobsters, Trigraplathons and other tasty aliens,

As a qualified teacher, he has run a number of workshops in schools and is the founder of CHINDI, the Chichester based group of independent authors. Cornish Writer of the year 2018, he actually hails from Wales.

For more information visit:
www.creaturesofchichester.com

Side by Side

by Alan Readman

Stille nacht, heilige nacht.

The words were strange to their uncultured ears.

Alles schläft, einsam wacht.

Yet there was no mistaking the melody.

For a few precious moments their minds were transported from that loathsome place, back to the village church in Sussex, where as boys they would sit, side by side, Sunday after Sunday, in their choir stalls of polished oak.

Suddenly, the scene was illuminated. The gunners had fired up star shells, which burst in the night sky, igniting magnesium flares. And for a time, No Man's Land was transformed, as bright as the light of day.

Ben whispered to his brother for fear a harsher tone might disturb the magic of the moment.

"Over there, Sam, on the other side, look, they've lit fires, all along the top of the trench. They're glowing like little beacons. Don't that remind you of them lamps they light back home in the village square?"

Sam hesitated for a time before answering, until he understood the full meaning of the scene before them. Only then did he reply.

"Yes, Ben, I see 'em alright. *'All is calm. All is bright'*. They're telling us it's Christmas Eve."

As their eyes adjusted further, they saw the Germans, some of them, sitting on their parapet, and now joining in the carol, led by the tenor who had begun the singing.

His voice, pure, ethereal, seemed to them to be of another world. Incongruous even, coming as it did from a fighting man, standing alone, in the grey-green uniform of the Kaiser's Army, on a battlefield on the Western Front.

Perhaps for that reason it transfixed them and filled them both with a sense of spiritual peace that they had feared the world had forever forfeited through the ghastly perversity of this war. And on that silent night, that holy night, the two brothers embraced each other and wept the tears of men who had stared into the abyss but now saw the promise of hope restored.

In some ways they were the most unlikely of brothers. Villagers had often remarked on that as they watched them growing up. Ben, twelve months the elder, was taller and stronger, full of life, always ready for adventure, the one who climbed the trees for birds' eggs and led the scrumping forays in the orchard. Sam was small for his age, the consequence of a lingering fever in infancy, and quieter in his ways, more withdrawn, a 'sensitive soul', his mother said.

Yet their brotherly love and their companionship were deeply rooted. Ben fought their battles in the school playground while Sam helped his brother with the homework he usually found so difficult.

Their shared delight was in the great outdoors, when, beneath a Sussex sky, they would stroll down a country lane or along a meandering riverbank, side by side, rejoicing in the simple joys of nature.

Together, they might hitch a ride on the carrier's cart to Arundel, to the Black Rabbit at the end of Mill Lane. There they would explore the reed beds, hoping to catch a fleeting glimpse of a kingfisher, darting down from its riverside perch to hunt its prey, or to hear the booming call of a bittern hiding amongst the tall rushes by the water's edge.

The vicar accosted their mother at the church door one Sunday morning.

"Those two boys of yours, Mrs Hardy, its plain to see they've a deep love for these parts, they know the ways of the land and the seasons better than most their age. They'll make you proud one day." She pondered these words and treasured them.

They would on occasions truant from school, helping in the harvest fields or beating for the shoot on the Duke's estate. It was rare they quarrelled, but they did over that. Ben welcomed the shooting season, enjoyed the spectacle and the thrill. Sam loved the regal beauty of the pheasants, hated the slaughter, and wondered why the witless birds didn't fly back into the woods rather than across the fields to the guns, as if drawn to their fate by some irresistible force.

Yet when his own time came he didn't flinch.

It was their curiosity about the wider world that took them away from the Sussex Downs and the banks of the River Arun.

"Are you sure about this?" their form teacher asked when they told him of their plans on their last day at the school. "I would have wagered you two would live out your lives in this village."

"Well, sir, you see, Sam and me, we want to follow our Dad. He told us tales when we were little of faraway places, like India and South Africa. Said we'd never see such sights if we didn't take the King's shilling, like he did. We promised him, just before he passed away, that if we did, we'd join his old regiment, no other. And that's what we're planning to do, sir, just as soon as we're old enough."

They revelled in the long months of training, the camaraderie of the platoon, the route marches through the English countryside, side by side, singing along the way the regimental marching songs of old. And when war came, there was excitement back then, bravado, born of a wave of patriotism and high spirits, a deeply felt compulsion to fight for a just and godly cause.

"Action at last, Sam. A chance for some real fighting. Show that Kaiser what we British lads are made of. Teach them marauders a lesson or two they won't forget. Vicar says it'll all be over by Christmas. Let's hope the battalion gets out there soon. We don't want to miss it. Bet our Jack will be green with envy."

Indeed he was, for their younger brother was almost seventeen, looked older most said, and had grown restless with the mundane routine of village life, alone now in the cottage with his mother and sisters.

He had seen the posters all over Chichester, on the windows of the *Observer* office and the hoardings outside the railway station, on the inner pillar of the Cross and the walls of Shippam's factory in East Street. Everywhere he looked, the beckoning finger of Lord Kitchener seemed to be pointing directly at him. He listened to the excited chatter of the other Shippam's lads, all anxious to join the big adventure and do their bit for King and Country, and he too felt compelled to respond to the call to arms.

He came home from the factory one day to find his mother, with Elsie and Annie, stirring the Christmas pudding.

When they were alone he told her of the recruiting meeting he'd been to in the Drill Hall. The rousing speeches and the raucous cheering. The dashing young officers from the Barracks with their open-top cars.

"They say they're going to form a battalion all of Sussex lads, Mum. To train and fight together. Colonel Osborn was there from the Royal Sussex. He said he wants a thousand men to join him. A couple of chaps from Shippam's signed up right there and then. When everyone started singing 'Sussex by the Sea' I felt a thrill inside me. I want to be out there, too, Mum, like Ben and Sam. I'll miss all the fun if I leave it too long."

He dodged a cuff around the ear. "Fun, you think war is fun! That's fools' talk. Don't you dare think of going to any more of them meetings. You're too young to join the army anyway. Well, I'll tell you one thing, Jack, I'm not going to let all this war business spoil Christmas for the girls. It wouldn't be fair on them. It's bad enough with your brothers being away from home for so long. I'm not going to have you going off as well. I've given two sons to the King. I'm not going to give him a third. You're needed at home, you are, my lad."

As the weeks passed by, and the war news in the local paper became more depressing, she felt her appetite for festive cheer diminish. But it was Christmas time and for her daughters' sakes she busied herself with the usual preparations. There was a tree and holly for the parlour from the estate, and the lady at the big house brought them a pheasant and a plum loaf. The girls decorated the room with the paper chains they'd made at school and their mother invited to their Christmas table the next-door neighbours whose only son was still missing at Ypres.

The vicar at the Christmas morning service read out the names of those from the village who had answered the call and he spoke of the noble duty that had drawn them away from their homes. All the while, as he preached his sermon, mothers in the congregation, like her, stared through tearful eyes at the empty spaces in the choir stalls and in the pews. They bit their lips and wondered what this special time held in store for their sons across the Channel.

The two brothers clapped and cheered the German tenor.

"Can you believe what we've just seen, Ben? Have you ever heard a better performance of 'Silent Night' than that? And in No Man's Land of all places!"

The British lads responded, if not in quality then at least in spirit, with a rousing rendition of 'Tipperary'.

Voices began to call out from all along the enemy trenches, clear and sharp, cutting through the chill air of that still and frosty night.

"Merry Christmas, Tommy. Don't shoot. We're friends tonight."

Then, one by one, hesitatingly at first, then with greater boldness, soldiers from both sides began to put down their rifles and make their way out into the open expanse of No Man's Land.

There, they shook hands, embraced each other, laughed, and exchanged cigarettes, proud and happy that they, from the lowly rank and file, had found a way of stopping the madness of war and sharing the peace of Christmas Eve.

A tall, fair-haired boy, of about their own age, they thought, came towards them, smiled in greeting, and offered his hand. The older brother grinned in response, and warmly shook his hand, just as if they were old friends meeting again in a country pub after a long absence.

"Hello, my name is Ben. I'm sorry I don't speak German. This is Sam, my brother, he's much cleverer than me but he doesn't know any German either. We didn't learn it in the village school, you see, back home in Sussex."

"Ja, but tonight that is no trouble, my friend. You see, I speak English. Before this all began, I live in London for a year, learning to be a chef in one of your best hotels. They call it the Ritz. You've heard of it, no? When I left, they tell me I speak English good, like a Cockney, I think you say. So we can talk together, yes."

Sam laughed and clapped him on the back. "Yes, we are all friends tonight. It's Christmas. Look, here in my pocket, I have a photograph. This is our mother, and that's Elsie and that one's little Annie, they're our sisters. And you, tell us *your* name. Perhaps, when this is all over, we can all meet together, our families, in your Ritz Hotel?"

Neither shell nor shot was fired that night. Next morning, on Christmas Day, again the two sides approached each other in No Man's Land. Rum rations were shared and in return the Tommies tasted schnapps for the first time.

The two brothers were on sentry duty, as fate would have it, but from the fire-step of the trench they at least had a grandstand view of the proceedings.

"Ben, look, over there, they've got a ball. Wherever did that come from? Can you see? They're having a kick-about. For heaven's sake, Ben, there's a football match going on out there! In No Man's Land. On Christmas Day. England against Germany! Can you believe your eyes?"

The tree and decorations had been taken down by the time the letter arrived. 'From your ever-loving son and brother'. She wiped away a tear as she read it to them at the breakfast table.

"It's from Sam. Look, girls, there's kisses for you both at the end. He says that he and Ben were thinking of us all on Christmas Day and missed the village and the church. But he wants us to know that they still had a wonderful Christmas. They got the scarves and mittens I knitted. And he thanks you for the cards you made. Oh, and he says all the soldiers got little brass boxes from Princess Mary, that's the King's daughter, with chocolate and cigarettes inside. And, my goodness, listen to this, they sang carols and made pals with a German boy called Stefan. He says it was a magical moment."

Annie took the letter from her mother and kissed her brother's name. "Does that mean we're friends again with the Germans, Mum? Is that the end of the war? Oh, Mum, will Sam and Ben be home soon? Tomorrow, do you think?"

She smiled gently as she looked down on her two girls. "I don't know, my darlings, but let's hope and pray you're right. At least we do know they're both safe today."

Christmas seemed a lifetime ago.

The barrage that morning was deafening. The artillery on each side of the front line seemed intent on outdoing the other. Like a satanic exchange of hate. As if the sanity that had been restored on Christmas Eve had visited this place and turned away in despair, abandoning them all to their fates.

Sam's nerves got the better of him and for a time he cowered in the trench, shaking from head to foot, until Ben steadied him, reminding his brother that they were doing this for the people and places back home.

An officer's whistle blew and over the top they went, side by side. Sam saw the horizon before them break into a jagged line of red flame, the air around them at once alive with zipping bullets and bursting shrapnel, the ground shuddering with the relentless bombardment. Like lambs to the slaughter they pressed on. Like pheasants to the guns.

When he regained consciousness, hours later, he had no recollection of the advance, or the explosion. He found himself slumped within a shell hole, filled deeply by the incessant rain, a crater of cloying mud dragging his aching limbs down into the filthy water.

A faint sigh escaped the lips of the figure by his side. Ben at least was alive. The bullet had entered his body via his shoulder but where it had gone next there was no telling. Sam made his decision. If his life was to be saved, he must get his brother back to their trenches now, before the light of dawn.

It was no easy matter to lift him onto his back. No one knew how he did it, where the strength came from, to crawl across those few hundred yards of No Man's Land. When he reached the parapet of their trench, willing hands reached out to help. He didn't notice their glances, one to another, as they took down the lifeless body of his brother. He straightened and stretched. He didn't hear the crack of the sniper's bullet or feel its impact as it smashed into his skull.

It was just two short weeks after Christmas when the post office boy delivered the telegrams. To a cottage in a Sussex village, a cottage with an opened letter lying on a kitchen table.

For his sermon that Sunday, the vicar took as his text John 15, 'Greater love hath no man than this, that a man lay down his life for his friend'. Or his brother.

Two simple wooden crosses marked the spot where they buried the bodies. Side by side.

Not in a quiet churchyard in a sleepy village nestling in the Sussex Downs. But on a battlefield in a faraway place where they would dream for all eternity of happy times, of friendship grasped, of the spirit of Christmas, all thought of evil cast away.

Alan Readman

Alan Readman comes from Grimsby but has lived most of his life in Bognor and Felpham. A graduate of Sheffield University, where he studied Economic History, he worked as an archivist first at Lincolnshire Archives Office and later West Sussex Record Office, retiring from the latter as County Archivist in 2013.

During his career he wrote and lectured on local, military and family history but recently his interest has turned to fiction writing, with the help of U3A creative writing courses. This is his second short story to be published, the first being 'A Journey Of Discovery' earlier this year which appears in the Bognor Regis Write Club anthology: *'Meet The Winners'*.

The Christmas Present

by Maralyn Green

In the Inglenook, way down the Pagham Road, Bertha was warming her ample posterior by the open log fire, having just announced that she was thinking of getting a new cleaner, called Robert. It was going to be a special Christmas present for herself.

"But whatever's happened to Jill?" burst out Mavis, her chins quivering in surprise. We all knew that Jill had been cleaning and cooking for Bertha since time immemorial, or at least since her husband, Percy, had passed out in the kitchen one day and wasn't even revived by the smell of his spicy sausages burning.

"Well, it's a real shame, but Jill was getting past it," admitted Bertha, casting a guilty look down at her brand-new ankle above her designer shoes. Even so, we old girls nodded in silent sisterhood with Jill, for few could afford the thumping cost of all the many replacement body parts now on offer.

The six of us had gravitated to Sussex from various places many moons ago on our retirements and had found our way to the stretch of coast around Bognor Regis. Part of the magnet pulling us all south had been our enjoyment of the invigorating sea air, the long sunshine hours and the total lack of hills when on previous visits. We had gradually made each other's acquaintance at church, the W.I. or luncheon clubs and in time had become a support group for each other. Over the years, with age creeping ever more into us, our activities had dwindled to meeting once a week in various local pubs to reminisce over long-lost youth, amazingly seven or eight decades ago, and to set the modern world to rights. So, when we heard the news about Bertha's Jill, we all had to have another Martini as we were only too familiar with the nagging aches and seemingly inevitable pains that afflicted one as the years passed. Indeed, when one of us could drum up a new spasm or twinge, we always commiserated with feeling and curiosity ... and another drink!

"But a Robert?" said Gertie, straightening her new wig, which had fooled none of us as we'd seen her sport so many others, "I've heard it's a bit expensive?"

"Well, as you know, Percy left me properly provided for," divulged Bertha with a wink that stuck her over-mascaraed eyelashes together briefly. Yes, Percy had certainly spoilt his wife: we'd all long ago guessed that those exquisitely set diamond rings and chunky golden necklaces, a bit outré for daytime wear, were not out of Woolworths ... and that's long gone now! Bertha continued, with both eyes now open, "So I thought why not treat myself this Christmas, who else will nowadays, not Percy bless his soul. I might as well get myself something I really want that won't wear out." No one said a word, and it was left to Gertie to raise her greying eyebrows, what was left of them, which aptly demonstrated all our feelings.

Anyway, we all wished each other a happy and warm Christmas, though truth to tell the Christmas holidays couldn't go by fast enough. Those of us who were heading off to visit family, or were being wheeled and spoon-fed kindness by relatives of all ages and hopefully not yet spoon fed our dinners, well, we couldn't wait to get back to our Bognor haunts and hear how Bertha's Christmas had transpired. We had heard nothing so we were all agog for news, that is, as agog as octogenarians can get, and which, surprisingly, turned out to be most energising in a sedentary way.

Early on the Sunday after Christmas, we all gathered inside The Waverley near the Promenade in Bognor, arriving by our various means of walking stick, bus or being dropped off by our carers, and sat in anticipation of Bertha's arrival. In readiness, we had commandeered the tables by the windows with, supposedly, the best beach view, even if that was ten tons of pebbles on buried sand, and perhaps a glimpse of the waves at low tide. With delicacy, we sipped our Pinot Grigios as we waited for Bertha, one neck or another occasionally craning to see which way she would come. Finally Bertha's new driverless car arrived and we all watched as she manoeuvred herself from its roomy confines, wearing the most enviable emerald green woollen coat and then, to our surprise, almost dragged herself into the pub not caring if her silver suede, slip-on shoes got scuffed in the process.

"So Bertha," enquired Mavis, leaning forward and watching impatiently as Bertha collapsed with unaccustomed heaviness and a strange lack of finesse into a chair, "We all want to know how you've got on with Robert."

Bertha took a good look around at us all, her eyes rather more tired and heavy lidded than usual. "Robert", she breathed, saying his name so slowly that it sounded more like a French *Robair*, and then her breathing became a touch laboured.   Finally she gained some control and continued, "Oh just adorable …. he does everything you want … and more."

There was a pause. We sat in silence. Surely there was more detail than that? Bertha gazed at our eager faces, and maybe she smiled, and, looking back, maybe it was a secret joke that amused her. Then, with the occasional breathy pause, she surprised us by saying, "Really I do feel most selfish having Robert all to myself. I have been wondering if each of you might like to have him for a day this coming week. A kind of belated Christmas present from me. What do you think?"

We protested, rather weakly, I have to confess. Bertha insisted, saying her house was sparkling, and it was making her feel rather worn out. So, somewhat hastily and in case Bertha changed her mind, a rota was organised and it was agreed that Robert would be at each of our houses in turn at 9am and finish by 6pm, having looked after us and our house for the day.

My turn was last, probably because I lived the furthest away in North Mundham. I was very comfortable there in my cosy cottage: *bijou* the estate agent had said and it truly was a gem. The village was so convenient for popping in to Bognor or Chichester by bus that I never felt lonely or stranded. However, I had my fingers firmly crossed that it wouldn't be too far for Robert. You see, I had been waiting all week, filled with such eager anticipation that all those fiddly, dusty corners, out-of-reach cobwebs, slightly grubby cupboard doors and less than pristine woodwork would finally be cleaned, as I had heard from the others that Robert was indefatigable and aimed to please.

Finally the day arrived and, when the doorbell rang, I shuffled to the door. I had put on one of my comfortable dresses, well-worn yet offering good arm and knee coverage and had looked critically at my hair in the mirror for several seconds before deciding, once again, that there was not much to be done with the thinning strands remaining. So, feeling satisfied that I looked presentable enough, I opened the door. Robert stood there, the most good-looking young man to have rung my doorbell for a long, long time. To say tall, dark and handsome was such a cliché, but he really was. In my opinion, he couldn't have been made any better. Bertha had chosen well and she must have paid a lot for him. He looked so real … I mean human.

Robert handed me a small bouquet of delicately scented red roses, all the time looking kindly into my eyes. I almost missed what he said next in his deep husky voice, yet I recovered in time to hear "Have I the pleasure of addressing Griselda?" Gosh, my name had never sounded so delightful and, with his slight accent, I felt wobbly and weak at the knees. Now, I accept that at my age such frailties are not unknown, but this really was different. For you see, your brain might know Robert was a robot, but your eyes deceived you every time you looked at him.

Robert helped me back through the hall to my armchair in the lounge, settled me down, asked if I'd had breakfast and disappeared. I was still feeling a bit dazed with my good fortune when he returned with those wonderful roses in a vase, a pot of Earl Grey tea, and a cooked breakfast daintily arranged on a tray. The morning passed by in the proverbial whirl as Robert really did seem to fly around the house, but always popping in to check that I had everything I wanted and was OK. So kind, so very comforting and, dare I say it, intoxicating, to have a man in the house wanting to please you. When lunchtime came, it was no different. To my old, unbelieving eyes, Robert had transformed my little dining room into something akin to The Ritz, it only lacked a chandelier, but to compensate I did have the most attractive and attentive waiter. On the table was my favourite meal of bangers and mash, or as Robert beautifully said "*Saucisses et purée de pommes de terre*", with broccoli florets on the side, definitely not *al dente*, and a glass of rosé wine. Where had he got it all from? How had he known?

Puzzling it all out was far too tiring, and after a short post-prandial doze, nestled in amongst my sofa cushions, … well, I at least thought it was a short nap, even if the mantelpiece clock told differently, Robert returned to the lounge. He wished me a Happy Christmas. I didn't like to tell him that was nearly two weeks ago now, but maybe nobody had changed his program, and he did say it so nicely. Somehow he put on some music, then bowed low like a true gentleman and asked me if I would care to dance. Sadly, I told him I could no longer do so, however, he decided otherwise and soon I was twirling and waltzing around the room, even if Robert's strong arms held me high so my feet hardly touched the floor. It was giddying but wonderful.

Oh, we danced and danced as the music changed from one song to another, and I felt young again and with that tingly feeling of being adored. Yes, I knew it was only Robert, I knew it was all make-believe, a computerised programme set to please the customer, a robot who wasn't bothered in the slightest by my many wrinkles, straggly white hair and hairy chin, yet still my emotions were all a-flutter. This old lady wanted her last taste of romance to last just a little bit longer, but eventually I had to protest that I was becoming pretty puffed. I realised now how Bertha must have felt, tired out by all this dancing every day, or so I thought. Robert gently came to a halt, whispered how wonderful I was, then looked at me quizzically. Would I like my Christmas present now? I smiled shyly, as once my younger self had done, and managed to bring my eyes up to meet his perfect azure ones. Even while my heart fluttered in anticipation, he picked me up, with so much care, and headed for the stairs.

Of course, I would dearly love to say that, after all the heady romancing, we spent a fabulous night of unbridled passion, but unfortunately that did not happen. No, after a very promising preamble, Robert had completely conked out and I just couldn't figure out how to plug him in for a recharge. As Bertha later said, with her arm tightly around Robert, at least the house was sparkling clean!

Maralyn Green

Maralyn Green is a published non-fiction writer, and now also enjoys writing fiction stories of all types and lengths. She is a member of the Bognor Regis Write Club and has also recently begun to have some of her short stories published.

Moon Shadows

by Bruce Macfarlane

The night before Christmas is not the best time of the year for your car to break down, with no phone signal, on a lonely country lane in deepest Sussex.

After my fourth attempt to start the engine the electrics died completely. Black. Pitch black. Not even a glow from the dashboard. After a while, my eyes became accustomed to the darkness, and through the windscreen I could just make out the sunken road, its banks lined with overhanging trees.

I needed a light. I searched through the car, and with relief, found my old bicycle lamp in the glove box and switched it on. The breath from my exertions in the cooling air had formed an opaque mist on the windows, which in the torch light seemed to enclose the car around me like a tomb. I quickly wiped the windscreen with my hand to see out, and to my horror, saw a distorted face staring back at me!

It took a second to realise it was my own illuminated reflection, and a little longer for my heart to stop racing.

I looked at the dead dashboard again and, swearing heavily, I tried once more to start the engine. Nothing. So, I decided to get out and find some help.

An ice-cold wind hit me which blew swirls of dead leaves into the car. I shut the door and swung the lamp around to get my bearings, but could see nothing except the tarmac road and the white fingers of naked beech roots climbing up the banks. As I moved away from the car I noticed a strange light bathe the road, and looking up, saw through the swaying black tendrils of the trees, a full moon racing across the sky between fleece-white, ragged clouds.

Which way? I had not seen a house for miles since crossing the old stone bridge at Stedham. Reasoning that there had to be one soon, I grabbed my coat from the car and took the direction I had been driving. As I walked along the road, glistening patches of frost appeared and disappeared between the moon shadows cast by the trees. After about a hundred yards, the shifting black shapes caused by the torch light unnerved me, and I turned off the lamp and let the moon guide me.

It was then I saw the white signpost.

A woman was standing next to it in a hooded cloak. Its colour, if it had any, was washed away by the moon. Trying not to frighten her, I shouted. "Hello!" But she didn't hear me in the wind. I approached closer and tried again. "Excuse me, but my car's broken down."

She turned. Her face was pale in the moonlight, but her eyes were soft and strangely welcoming.

"Oh, that often happens here," she said with a smile.

"I see. Is there a house round here where I could get help?"

"Perhaps at Iping but they'll all be abed, for the moon is up and they'll want to be asleep when he arrives. Mine is nearer if you wish."

And without another word she turned onto a footpath I hadn't seen and disappeared.

Seeing nothing else to do, I followed.

It was more of a deer track than a footpath. I chased after her with my torch, trying to avoid the overhead branches and tripping on hidden roots. When I eventually caught up with her, I said, "Do you live close to here?"

"Of sorts." she replied, "But when the moon is here it is easier to stay."

"What do you mean?"

'It is the light that helps. What do you need?"

"I want to phone a garage."

"Oh, you shouldn't worry about that. I am sure it will all be better in the morning."

But before I could ask what she meant I heard the tinkling of bells, far off beyond the woods. She turned in its direction and said, "We must make haste if we are to get home before the moon sets. You can see it is in a hurry tonight."

I looked up. It did indeed seem to be in a hurry.

As I followed her along the path I heard, almost muffled by the wind, the faint sound of bells again. It seemed to be coming from above the trees and had a strangely familiar jangling rhythm, but when I looked up I saw nothing but the moon darting between the swaying branches.

The frosted air was seeping through my coat and I began to wonder why I'd let myself follow her down the path instead of going to Iping. Then, just when I had almost made up my mind to turn back and take my chances on the road, I saw a light through the trees.

"Is that your house?" I said.

"It might be. Let me see."

She looked up at the moon. "Yes, that seems to be about right."

The cottage was old, with flint walls and Sussex tiling. By the porch, lit by twinkling fairy lamps, a window glowed with the light of a flickering fire. In the cold it seemed homely and welcoming. She went up to the door, opened it, then turning to me, said, "Quickly, come in, he is nearly here!"

I found myself in a single living room with white plaster walls and in the centre an old wooden table with two large plates. On the stove by the window, was a large skillet from which came the delicious aroma of roasting meat and chestnuts.

She removed her cloak, revealing a long red and gold dress embroidered with dancing hares entwined with wildflowers and green vines.

"That is beautiful." I said.

"Thank you." She smiled with pleasure and her eyes met mine. Soft familiar eyes that drew me to her. In the light of the fire her face momentarily reminded me of someone or something from a time past. But before I could think what it was she went over to the stove, bent over the skillet and said, "Ah, dinner is ready. Now sit down and I'll pour you some wine."

"Who's the other plate for?" I said.

"For you."

"You knew I was coming?"

"Not always. It depends on the light."

She placed the roasted meat on a board and brought it to the table.

"There, perfect and just in time. Do you want to carve? You always like to."

"OK, so what's going on?" I said, "You appear out of nowhere and then bring me here as though it was the most natural thing in the world."

"I didn't bring you. You came of your own accord. And to answer your question: have you forgotten I am your wife?"

"What?"

"Oh dear. You don't remember, do you? You are always surprised to see me. Well, what must be said must be said again."

Coming up close to me she tentatively placed her hand on my shoulder. "We were in the car driving home."

Her hand tightened on my shoulder. "You had a heart attack. You died a year ago."

I looked up in disbelief. "Died! What do you mean?"

"I tried to save you - but I couldn't, and I ran down the road for help. Then when I got to the signpost, I saw you in the moonlight coming towards me. I was so frightened. I thought you had died. Oh, the relief to see you! But you didn't recognise me. I thought you had amnesia from the accident, so I brought you home and put you to bed, but in the morning when I woke, you were gone."

"What are you talking about?"

"That's all I remember. Each full moon I find myself waiting for you at the signpost and if the light is right you come to me. Not always. Sometimes you recognise me. Other times, well, like now. It took a while before I realised that I had died in the car as well."

"This is ridiculous. I don't know what you're playing at. You're mad - I'm going!"

As I tried to leave, she grabbed my arm. "You have said that many times. But you always return."

I pulled her hand roughly away, ignoring the pleading look in her eyes, and ran out of the house without looking back, and down the path.

The full moon was now low in the sky and it was getting darker. A hanging blackthorn branch tore at my coat and, as I tried to remove it in the torch light, a sudden thought came to me. If the moon was setting, then it was nearly dawn. Impossible! I'd only left the car about half an hour ago. I checked my watch. A quarter to midnight. So the moon should have been overhead! What was going on? But my only thought now was to escape this madness and find the local village she said was nearby.

Eventually, I found the road and ran to the signpost expecting to find the direction to Iping. But its three white fingers were blank! I decided to go back to my car in the hope the engine would start again.

To my relief it was still there, parked in a layby and covered in white frost. But as I approached it I noticed there was something wrong. Very wrong. One tyre was flat and the windscreen was smashed. The silver-blue paint was flaking with rust and covered in dead leaves and debris. I checked the number plate. It was definitely my car. I tried the door. It was jammed. I yanked it again and it opened, revealing in the torch light an old bird's nest on the seat. I shut the door quickly. My back shivered with a cold, clammy sweat.

Then her words hit me like a bolt. "You died a year ago."

And as if to reinforce those awful words a bough creaked and cracked in the wind above me and fell with a crunch on the car.

I ran like the wind back down the road.

The moon had nearly set and I could hear that tinkling sound again. It was getting louder and closer behind me. I looked back and nearly jumped out of my skin as a group of heavily antlered deer leapt silently out of the trees, closely followed by what seemed to be an open carriage and vanished into the darkness. I shook my head in disbelief. I wanted nothing more than to be out of these woods and somewhere safe and warm. If the demons of hell had been behind me I could not have run faster. At the signpost, I dived into the undergrowth looking for the footpath. I hacked at the branches, stumbling on roots in panic. Moon shadows leapt towards me like dead hands trying to draw me from the path. Finally, to my relief, I saw the light of the cottage again.

She was standing at the open porch door, lit by the fairy lamps which cast coloured patterns on her dress. It may have been the cold playing tricks on my eyes but, just for a moment, their flickering glow seemed to bring the embroidered hares to life. Before I could catch my breath to speak, she said, "I knew you would come back." And she wrapped her arms around me. For only a second I hesitated, then I returned her embrace and a familiar fragrance washed over me. I knew who she was.

"Now come in, my love." she whispered, "Don't be scared. We have the whole night together again."

I entered in a daze and removed my coat to feel the warmth of the fire. Then I slowly walked over to the table, my heart still racing from my flight and sat down.

She brought her chair round and sat next to me. Her hand grasped mine and I felt an immense calm. The wind ceased to play on the windows and a strange silence and stillness pervaded the room. Even the flickering shadows cast by the fire seemed to fade away into nothingness. I sat mesmerised as my memory of her slowly returned and I immersed myself in its joy.

A noise outside broke my reverie. The sound of many hooves and tinkling bells, then silence...then footsteps, slow, measured footsteps, approaching on the gravel path. The footsteps stopped. Silence. Then three knocks on the door accompanied by a jolly laugh, as familiar as childhood.

I turned towards the door then back to her "Please don't tell me..." I stuttered in disbelief "Is that who I think it is?"

"Yes." She whispered. "I wished for you and he brought you to me. My Christmas present. Now fetch that warm mead and mince pie by the fire. I think he deserves a treat. Don't you?"

Bruce Macfarlane

Bruce Macfarlane is a retired health physicist living with his wife on the south coast of England, just a few minutes' walk from the sea. When he's not researching King Arthur, he's rambling on the South Downs with his wife and friends trying to remember all the names of the flowers his wife has identified.

A life of writing scientific reports and reading early science fiction, especially the genre of time travel, such as the works of Anderson, Simak and Wells encouraged him to start writing his own novels about the adventures of a modern man and a Victorian lady who meet at a cricket match in 1873.

His 'Time Travel Diaries' have been described by Ink Magazine as "Tom Holt meets P.G. Wodehouse meets Philip K. Dick meets Fortean Times."

You can find out more about his books on his blog at:
timediaries.wordpress.com/

Christmas Spirit
by Carol Thomas

When she had taken on an allotment in December, Ellie thought the weather would be her greatest challenge. Pulling her woolly hat down over her ears, folding her arms against the cold, and taking in the sight before her, she realised she had been mistaken.

The plot was overgrown with untended plants, long grass and brambles. The gnarly fruit trees were covered in lichen – a yield of edible fruit a thing of their past. Nature had claimed the land back, and while she could see the beauty in it, the plot was in no fit state to supply her with the fresh fruit and vegetables she had envisaged. Looking across at the bit of land she could now call her own, she knew it was going to take a lot of work, and quite some time before she would see the literal fruits of her labour. But she had waited so long for the opportunity she didn't care.

"You'll soon have it set to rights."

Ellie jumped as she turned to see an elderly lady, hunched into her coat, her nose and mouth covered by a woollen scarf. "I hope so." Ellie smiled.

"Fresh air and exercise, it's the perfect cure for a broken heart," the woman continued.

About to refute the fact she had a broken heart, Ellie saw the kindness in the woman's milky-blue eyes and smiled. "Thank you." Deciding to change the subject, she looked across the allotment. "Do you have an ..." but her words trailed off, disappearing in wisps of smoke into the cold air, as she realised the woman was making her way back down the uneven path.

Watching her go, Ellie thought about what the woman had said - her sentiment was more apt than she could have known. While Ellie's ex-husband had a new wife and a new life in London, Ellie had decided to make the move she had long dreamt of, to the West Sussex countryside. After securing herself a small cottage with a view of the rolling South Downs, Ellie had taken on an allotment, thinking the fresh air and exercise, as much as the homegrown produce, would do her good.

Zipping up her jacket against the cold, Ellie looked at the weathered shed. Despite its current state, it had clearly been well loved in the past. The blue door showed layers of paint, while forget-me-not blue curtains hung in the window. Ellie smiled at a wooden plaque above the door that read 'weed 'em and reap'.

Taking the key from her pocket, she lifted the rusty padlock, orange staining her gloves as she attempted to push the key into the hole. After a little wiggling, it slipped into place, took purchase and turned, releasing the lock.

It felt strange opening somebody else's shed, but she had been advised that it and its contents came with the allotment. The previous owner had apparently insisted upon it. Looking inside, Ellie was transfixed. It was as if she had opened a portal to the past – a moment frozen in time.

A pale blue, well-loved gardening hat hung on a peg above a pair of green wellingtons, standing proudly just inside the door. A tarnished spoon and three mismatched mugs were on the wooden workbench, next to a small blue Calor gas stove and idle whistling kettle. A vintage Typhoo tea caddy, its lid slightly askew, was on a shelf above. Tools of all varieties were hung along the wall, each with their own place, some with small clods of soil long dried onto them, all with their wooden handles made shiny and smooth by use.

Ellie smiled as she caught sight of a little orange watering can. Written above it, in a child's script, were the words 'George's water can'. So the previous owner had a child, or grandchild perhaps? Certainly, a little helper – someone who took pride in their watering can having its own place in the shed.

Ellie thought about the moment the door had last been closed. The objects inside were rich with history, well-loved and precious despite their time-worn appearance. Memories were etched into the fabric of every item before her. She smiled, grateful to the previous owner who had passed it into her care, and felt more determined than ever to restore the plot and the shed to its former glory. Selecting several tools from the shed, Ellie decided that there was no better time to start than the present.

After three hours of hacking, digging, weeding and pruning, Ellie stopped to admire the stretch of ground she had cleared. It was barely a foot wide, but it ran the length of the allotment. The compost bin she discovered behind the shed was full, and she had prepared a bonfire heap, which she knew she would have to get permission from the council to light. Her sense of achievement far outweighed the size of the bit of land she had cleared, but it was a start. The exercise had been a good workout for body and soul; despite the chill air, Ellie felt hot and invigorated.

Deciding to call it a day and head home, she first selected some holly from the nearby hedgerow and placed it in a small trug she had found in the shed. Christmas was only two days away and creating garlands of holly seemed a fitting way to decorate a cottage in the countryside. Who needed high-end, overpriced ornaments when they had natural beauty all around them?

Happy with her morning's work, and pleased at the thought of entwining the holly with red ribbon, she placed the tools back in the shed. Just as she was about to lock the door, there came a clatter from inside. Ellie's heart leapt. Thinking she had perhaps not hung the tools correctly, she opened the door. Peering inside, her eyes met the wide-eyed gaze of a ginger cat, which had knocked the tea caddy from the shelf near the kettle. The cat stood motionless, apart from the flick of its tail. Ellie crouched to greet the feline intruder. Unsure at first, it looked at her, its marmalade-coloured eyes assessing her, its whiskers taut.

Waiting for the cat to make the first move, Ellie sat still, and spoke softly, "Hello, where have you come from?" Reading the cat's name from the disk on its collar she continued, "It's nice to meet you, Marmaduke."

The cat cocked its head.

"I thought I was all alone here." Ellie smiled. Like owning an allotment, having a pet had been another of her wishes low down on her ex-husband's list of priorities for them as a couple.

The cat sauntered towards her, his white paws silent on the wooden floor. As he reached her, he rubbed his head against her leg. Ellie stroked along his back – his body arching into her palm as he walked. When he'd passed by, and the tip of his tail left her hand, he circled to do it again, emitting a loud purring noise as he went.

After sitting with Marmaduke for some time, Ellie lifted him out of the shed. He didn't struggle and sat contentedly in her arms, allowing her to stroke behind his ears.

"Wow!"

Ellie jumped and turned to see who had spoken. Standing at the end of the path was a tall, dark-haired man, dressed in jeans, and an Aran jumper – revealing broad shoulders and toned muscles. She was sure she hadn't seen him in the village before; she would have remembered. She pushed her fingers through her hair and wiped the back of her hand across her forehead.

"He really likes you," the man spoke with an amused tone.

Ellie looked from the cat in her arms to the gaze of the man walking towards her. "Can I help you? I've just taken over here." She gestured to the strip of land she had cleared and then wished she hadn't; it really wasn't that much of an achievement.

The man stopped for a beat, taking in the sight of the allotment, before nodding towards the cat. "I hope you don't mind. Whenever he goes missing I know I'll find him here."

"Of course not." Ellie placed the cat on the ground.

The man bent to stroke Marmaduke, who circled between his legs. "This—" the man gestured to the allotment "—is his favourite place."

"He's welcome any time, he's been great company." As the words left her mouth, Ellie wished she hadn't made herself sound quite such a desperado in the company department.

The man looked at her, a hint of a smile tugging at his lips. "Perhaps if we swap numbers you could let me know when he's here."

Ellie felt heat rise in her cheeks, wondering if she would be crazy to swap numbers with a total stranger. But she was still relatively new to the area, and getting to know people was an essential part of settling into a new community, wasn't it? "OK!" she said, removing her phone from her pocket and going to her contacts list.

As the man told her his number, she typed it in, before asking his name.

"George," he replied.

"George?" Ellie giggled. "Not as in orange watering can, George?" The man before her was not at all what she had imagined when she had spotted the child's script in the shed.

"Ha, yes, is it still in there?" His eyes flicked to the open shed door.

"Yes, take a look if you like."

As George looked inside, he breathed a heavy sigh before turning to Ellie, his deep blue eyes glistening. "Sorry, it's just, it's been a long time."

Breaking the moment, Marmaduke meowed.

George picked him up. "I can see why you feel close to her here," he whispered before looking at Ellie. "Gran passed away almost a year ago, but she was one of those characters – so full of life it's hard to accept she's gone. And she loved it here. It was her haven after Grandad died."

Ellie looked at George, and the cat in his arms. "You're both welcome here, any time. Honestly." She turned and looked at the allotment. "Goodness knows I could do with the help."

"I'm not that great with plants, but I'd be happy to lend a hand clearing the land, between shifts."

"Shifts?"

"I'm a firefighter." He smiled.

"So you've got a big hose now then!" Ellie spoke before considering the implications of her words. "I meant instead of a watering can ... I didn't mean ..." She wished the ground would swallow her up, as she felt heat spread across her neck and cheeks.

George laughed. "It's fine, I knew what you meant." Placing Marmaduke down, George spotted the tea caddy the cat had knocked onto the shed floor and leaned in to pick it up. "I've visited Gran here as an adult too. I know what's in this."

"Tea?" Ellie asked.

George eased the lid off the caddy and took out a small bottle of whisky, as he stepped back outside the shed.

"Don't suppose you fancy a toast, do you?"

Beginning to feel the chill in the air, now that the warmth she felt from her earlier exertion was dissipating, Ellie welcomed the gesture. "Of course, to your gran?" she asked.

George thought for a moment. "No. Christmas is almost here—" he nodded towards Ellie's trug of holly and the robin redbreast that had aptly perched upon it "—and a new year is just around the corner, so how about ... new beginnings?"

Ellie picked up two of the mugs from the side in the shed. She wiped them out with a clean tissue from her pocket, before holding them steady while George poured the whisky. As he took his drink, their hands met for the briefest moment, and her cheeks coloured at the welcome sensation of his touch.

"To a merry Christmas, and new beginnings," he said, as they clinked the mugs together, meeting each other's gazes with a smile.

Ellie drank – the amber liquid slipping down easily, spreading warmth in its wake. As she went to replace the tea caddy on the shelf, she noticed a photograph it had been hiding, pinned with a single drawing pin into the shed wall. Ellie wiggled the pin out, holding the picture closer to get a better look. It was of the allotment. Its impressive crop of runner beans curling around their sticks, and neat rows of potatoes, spring cabbage and other vegetables were an inspiration. But it was the kind blue eyes of the woman at the side of the picture Ellie was drawn to.

"I haven't seen that picture of Gran for a long time," George said.

Ellie passed him the photograph. As he held it in his hand, she noticed the words written in a cursive script on the back: '*Fresh air and exercise, the perfect cure for a broken heart.*'

As her pulse quickened, Ellie looked at George, the cat at his feet, and the allotment she had waited so long for. "Merry Christmas and to new beginnings," she whispered into the empty shed, echoing their toast of moments before.

Carol Thomas

Carol Thomas writes contemporary romance, with relatable heroines and irresistible male leads. After self-publishing her debut novel, Crazy Over You, in 2015 she went on to gain a publishing contract, with Ruby Fiction, an imprint of the award-winning romance publishers Choc Lit.

Her subsequent romantic comedy novels, The Purrfect Pet Sitter and Maybe Baby, have both gained Amazon best-seller badges and have been described as "fun, romantic, heart-warming stories, filled with friendship and love!" Having lived in West Sussex her whole life, Carol takes inspiration from the local area, setting her novels in and around her hometown of Littlehampton.

Carol has had short stories published in previous Chindi collections, *Your Cat* magazine, and online via Choc Lit. Drawing on her fifteen-years-experience as a teacher, she also writes for children. Her picture book, Finding a Friend, is the tale of an adorable puppy in need of a home.

The Knucker's First Christmas
by Patricia Feinberg Stoner

A Knucker lived in Lyminster, a Knucker as old as time.

Long, long ago when the world was young and strange, ungainly creatures crawled from the primordial slime, the Knucker spread giant wings and soared into the sky. He looked about him at the pre-Cambrian landscape and watched with interest as life developed below.

The Knucker is a water dragon; he is both ancestor and cousin to the great dragons of China and Wales. But while their hides glow gold and fiery red and they belch fire and noxious gases, the Knucker's scales are silvery green and his breath can be as gentle as a young girl's kiss.

Legend has it that in times gone by the Knucker would ravage and terrorise the countryside, stealing sheep, carrying off maidens and terrifying ploughboys. It is said he held sway for thousands of years until a local lad fed him a poisoned pie and he perished.

The story is a calumny. The Knucker is a peaceable soul, wanting only to live in harmony with his neighbours, as we shall see.

One day, tired and saddened at being made a scapegoat by sheep thieves, absconding maidens and cowardly ploughboys, he decided to withdraw from the world. He found a deep, deep pool close by the Lyminster church of St Mary Magdalene, and there he would sleep for half the year.

Winter was not his time. When the days grew short and chill, and the moon turned from gold to silver, then the

Knucker would seek the shelter of his cave above the dark waters of his pool, deep beneath the earth, and sleep the cold season away.

It was summer that the Knucker loved. How he would dance on the soft winds under the moon, swooping with the owls and playing tag with the foxes as they hunted. Sometimes, on a summer midnight, a late-dallying courting couple would look up as a shadow flitted across the stars. The girl would tremble and cling closer to her swain, who would put a protecting arm around her and murmur, "Don't fret, lass, 'tis only the old Knucker, he won't do you no harm."

But on this Christmas Eve something woke him. The Knucker opened his eyes. A sweet noise, carried through the still air, perplexed and delighted him. 'Silent Night', he heard, uncomprehending, and 'In the Deep Midwinter'. The church was full for the midnight carol service. Candlelight flickered behind the stained-glass windows, casting hues of red and yellow, blue and green on the frost-rimed grass of the churchyard. Voices rose in harmony, rejoicing as they sang the traditional songs of Christmas.

The Knucker crept from his cave to listen. Above him, the icy stars were not the stars he knew, and he shivered in the unaccustomed chill. Slowly he unfolded his wings, shaking out the stiffness of his hibernation. He stood on tiptoe and with a mighty leap soared up into the sky, sailing above the spire as the midnight congregation spilled out into the churchyard.

Most grownups can't see the Knucker, but sometimes the very young can. A little girl in a red coat pointed and waved excitedly. Her parents shushed her, but the Knucker bowed to her gravely, and the little girl bowed back.

For a few moments the Knucker circled above the church, looking with interest at the unfamiliar winter skyscape. Spotting an owl he knew, he whiffled with delight and flew off to join her, but the owl, intent on her hunting, had no time to play.

In the distance, a wash of light caught the Knucker's eye. He flew out over the silent streets to the nearby village of Littlehampton, where the high street was ablaze with colour, noisy still with revellers at this late hour.

A Knucker can walk unseen when he wishes to. He folded back his giant wings and landed like a feather in the midst of the Christmas crowds. He walked unnoticed among them, but a baby in a pushchair saw him and waved her chubby fists. The Knucker's golden eyes looked into the child's blue ones; the baby giggled and kicked her feet, so that her mother smiled and fondled her head through the thick woolly cap.

An old man huddled in the doorway of Boots the Chemist, his arms clasped round a small brown and white mongrel, man and dog giving each other the comfort that the thin sleeping bag couldn't provide. The man slept as the Knucker stooped over them, but the little dog gave a yip of surprise, wagging his tail in welcome. The Knucker huffed the tiniest of huffs and the man sighed, relaxing in the sudden warmth that would remain with him all night. In the morning he would be woken by a young woman in a Salvation Army uniform, carrying coffee and a mince pie and a chewy bone for the dog.

Delicious smells floated in the air. The Knucker snuffed, warily: he remembered a long-ago smell, and a young lad offering him something that tasted exquisite but left him with crippling pains in his stomach. Could it be the same? No: this had spice in it, and succulent fruit, and the snap of brandy.

A group of young people were sharing something from a white box, laughing and jostling each other and eating. A little boy, under the reluctant watch of his elder sister, held out a sticky hand with the remains of a mince pie. The Knucker dipped his head: cautiously he lapped at the boy's palm, relishing the sweet-sharp taste of the pastry. Questioned by the group, the little boy said simply: "It's for the dragon," earning himself a burst of laughter and a rough cuddle from his sister. But the child knew what he had seen.

The Knucker flew on, exploring this unaccustomed winter town. Away from the high street all was quiet and seemingly deserted, the people celebrating in the centre of town or relaxing by their firesides, basking in the warm glow of anticipation.

Suddenly, from a darkened garden, a streak of light shot up, followed by a loud bang, and sparkled down in cascades of silver and blue and green. Enchanted, the Knucker drew in a deep breath and let fly a stream of green fire; he tumbled and somersaulted in the air as the fireworks crackled around him, adding his own lustre to the Christmas display.

When at last the fireworks were done, he went on his way; over Pier Road he flew, and out over the RNLI station to the river. The lifeboat was chugging homewards, the

63

crew chilled but content after a successful rescue. A small sailing dinghy, its hull painted a cheerful red but its one sail listing and tattered, bobbed along on tow behind the boat. Its skipper, old Pete, was well known to the crew: they had rescued him many a time after he had set out on a wave of optimism and brandy to sail to the Isle of Wight.

A festive evening in the Dolphin Inn had convinced Pete that this was the night he would finally achieve his ambition and make landfall at Cowes harbour. Now he sat cheerfully in the stern of the lifeboat, wrapped in a blanket, regaling the tired crew with sea shanties and Christmas pop songs and keeping time with flourishes of a half empty bottle of Courvoisier.

The Knucker bowed to the lifeboat and old Pete waved happily back, but whether he saw the dragon as it flew above him, or whether he was waving at some chimera of his own, we shall never know.

The Knucker chortled as the busy Arun rushed beneath him on an ebbing tide, and a strand of tinsel, caught in the river's swirl, glittered beneath the moon. He swooped to trail his toes in the turbulent water, startling a dreaming fish which had been swept into the harbour some twelve hours earlier.

Something wet and cold surprised him: he looked up to see a thousand silver flakes drifting down. For a long time he played with them, exulting in the icy air and laughing as the snowflakes sizzled on his tongue.

As the full moon drifted down towards the west, silvering in its descent, and one by one the lights went out in the streets below, the Knucker turned for home. The church of St Mary Magdalene was silent and dark, only a glimmer from guttering candles causing the angel in the rose window to shiver and flutter her wings gently. With a sigh of content, the Knucker sought the peace of his cave; turning round three times he settled and curled into a peaceful sleep.

The Knucker never woke at Christmas again. But sometimes he would stir and smile in his sleep at visions of coloured lights and warm smells, happy voices and excited laughter. And sometimes his tongue would dart out to catch a drifting snowflake.

Patricia Feinberg Stoner

Former journalist and Chindi member, Patricia Feinberg Stoner is a writer of humorous books set in the Languedoc: the memoir 'At Home in the Pays d'Oc', which won a Five Star award from One Stop Fiction, and a collection of short stories, 'Tales from the Pays d'Oc'. She has also published two books of comic verse: 'Paw Prints in the Butter' - a collection of cat poems - and 'The Little Book of Rude Limericks'.

She lives with her husband and a mad spaniel called Maisie in Rustington, West Sussex, where Michael Flanders encountered a gnu and the mobility scooter is king. Find her on Facebook at Paw Prints in the Butter and on Twitter @perdisma.

Pudding

by Lexi Rees

Melanie padded downstairs in her dressing-gown and surveyed the sea of packing boxes. Mug of tea in hand, she leaned back against the Aga, gently toasting her legs. Her phone buzzed, announcing the arrival of a text from her mum.

How's the unpacking? It's great you're in the house in time for Christmas.

Offering to host the family Christmas lunch had seemed like a good idea at the time – a chance to show off her chocolate-box cottage and to prove she was putting her life back together – but the place had been empty for years and the reality was less chocolate-box and more an ever-growing to-do list of leaks to fix, draughts to plug, and strange noises to identify. With her new job in a nearby gastropub starting in a few days, she had no idea how she was going to get through everything in time. A packet of mince pies caught her attention. Okay, not the ideal breakfast, but at least they were 'not just any mince pies' (according to the advert).

Her phone buzzed again.

Don't forget it's Stir-up Sunday.

Stir-up Sunday was an old family tradition where everyone took turns to stir the Christmas pudding and make a wish.

Just in case you haven't had time to go shopping yet, I'll bring the ingredients round.

Melanie caught her reflection in the mirror. Did she really look that rough? She ran her hands through her unbrushed hair and braced herself for another text, fearing the worst.

I've invited Pippa and the kids too.

Great. Not only was her hair a mess, but the cottage was a tip. This was not how she'd planned on seeing Pippa for the first time in a year. They'd been close as kids but had drifted apart when she'd gone to college. After graduating, her job had consumed almost every waking moment, so for the past few years they'd only seen each other at family gatherings. Then last Christmas, while Melanie's life had collapsed around her, losing first her job, then her boyfriend and, to cap it off, her beloved dog, Pippa had swanned around showing off her perfect family. Melanie had fumed silently all day, and not returned any of Pippa's calls or messages since. Despite all Melanie's hard work, she was still miles away from her dream of running her own restaurant, while Pippa did nothing except take staged photos yet had thousands of followers on social media. *Z-list*, Melanie thought, dumping the empty mug in the sink.

"Right, I can do this. But what should I do first?"

She opened the door to the kitchen cupboard. Well, not a cupboard exactly, this was a proper pantry, lined from floor to ceiling with shelves. Dreams of those same shelves stacked with home-made jams and jellies, topped by pretty gingham-wrapped lids and hand-written labels were, for now, just that – dreams. Today, it was more important that it had a door. Half an hour later she'd piled the shelves high with a higgledy-piggledy muddle of pots and pans and assorted baking utensils. She went to close the door to hide the mess, but the Aga kept the room cosy and the cool air from the tiny pantry window provided a welcome breeze. It'd have to remain slightly ajar or else she'd melt.

Just time for a quick shower, she thought. She was still towel-drying her hair when her mother arrived, laden down with shopping. Melanie laughed as she tipped out bags of currants, mixed peel and various other ingredients for the pudding.

"You do know we're not feeding the entire village, Mum?"

"Store cupboard essentials. They'll keep."

Melanie eyed the packet of suet suspiciously. Who actually used suet nowadays? Okay, so she wasn't vegan, not even really veggie, but still, it was hardly a store cupboard essential. Even pasta and couscous had been pushed to the side and her shelves brimmed with quinoa, freekeh and spelt. Her thoughts were interrupted by a cacophony of voices. Through the leaded kitchen window, she glimpsed her designer-clothed nephew and niece tearing up the path, followed by Pippa, looking distinctly un-mumsy in skinny grey jeans, a pale pink cashmere sweater and a cream-coloured faux-fur gilet. Never one to miss an opportunity for her lifestyle blog, Pippa fluffed her glossy hair and posed for a selfie in front of the cottage, the traditional Sussex brick and flint design providing an idyllic Country Life backdrop. Melanie took a deep breath and popped the kettle on.

As Pippa stepped into the hall, her eyes flicked right and left, assessing every inch. Melanie imagined her listing the flaws, 'The hall is narrow and dingy, the ceiling too low, the floorboards creak, the staircase dangerously steep ...'

Braced for a volley of criticism, Melanie smiled at her younger sister. Pippa beamed back at her. "It's gorgeous. I love it. So quaint and charming. It's totally you."

Melanie tried to decide if that last comment had a barb but decided she didn't care. Pippa was right, it was 'totally her'. It was everything she'd ever dreamed of.

"Where's Callum?" Although Callum was predictably good-looking and completed the family picture, she sensed he was rather bemused by this lifestyle and would have been quite happy to slob on the sofa in front of the TV with a pizza like a 'normal' person.

"He had to go to Zurich for work. He's got a very important meeting first thing tomorrow."

Conversation stalled, and Melanie busied herself with making two teas and a decaf espresso for Pippa. The kids sprinted round the cottage, yelling approval as they went. Ben was fascinated by the claw foot bath, while Sarah declared the sun-drenched window seat overlooking the garden to be 'the bestest reading spot ever'.

When it was time to prepare the Christmas pudding, Ben and Sarah bickered over whose turn it was to drop the lucky silver coin into the mixture, until Pippa persuaded them to do it together.

After everyone had stirred it and made their wish, Melanie poured the mixture into the ceramic pudding bowl, wrapped it in tinfoil, and tied it up with string. She half opened the pantry door, trying to hide the mess from her sister, and tried to slide it onto the highest shelf. The bowl caught on something and she stood on tiptoes to push it fully onto the shelf, dislodging a puff of dust. She made a mental note to get a small ladder and clean the shelf properly. Family tradition satisfied and shared, courtesy of Pippa, with the world via social media, Pippa whisked the kids off after as short a time as could be deemed decent.

The weeks in the run-up to Christmas passed in a whirlwind of activity. In just her second week at the gastropub, the head chef agreed to let Melanie experiment with some of the dishes. They peeked out of the kitchen to watch the customers tuck in, high-fiving as they practically licked the plates clean.

Melanie attended a festive wreath-making workshop at the local garden centre, and proudly pinned her slightly lopsided effort to the front door of the cottage, hoping it was robust enough to hold up to the windy weather. She wrapped garlands of ivy around the fireplace and up the bannister and covered every surface with candles and bowls of festive pot-pourri. The living tree left a trail of mud and pine needles as she dragged the heavy pot through to the sitting room. She wiped a bead of sweat from her forehead with the back of her hand and knelt in front of the tree to start decorating it. Three attempts later, the fairy lights still showed gaping holes. *How on earth does Pippa make everything look so perfect?*

She paused over the last box of decorations containing the cardboard angel and cotton-wool-ball snowman she and Pippa had made one afternoon many years ago, then propped them up in their places.

Christmas Eve saw Melanie whirling round the cottage, plumping cushions and arranging, then re-arranging, the baubles on the tree. Despite countless tweaks, the fairy lights still weren't evenly spread. She shoved tinsel into the gaps. It was nearly midnight before everything was ready and she collapsed into bed.

A loud crash tore her from her sleep. Burglars? She picked up a tennis racket and crept downstairs. As she tip-toed into the kitchen, her heart sank. There, on the pantry floor, surrounded by Christmas pudding and pottery shards, sat a large tabby cat, looking, at least by cat standards, exceptionally guilty.

Picking through the pudding mess, she spotted a bundle of papers, tied with a red ribbon. On the top of the bundle was an envelope. A smear of sticky crumbs ran across it. Delightful. She wiped the crumbs off. It was addressed to a Miss Agnes Woolley. The handwriting was exquisite, reminding her of the letters in the display cases at Arundel Castle. Melanie opened it, the thin paper crackling under her fingers.

My Dearest Agnes,

You may think I am foolish in my writing endeavours, yet I have had some small success with The Queene-Like Closet of which we may talk more at our luncheon. As 'tis likely be cold and wintry, I decide we shall eat a Sussex Pond Pudding. This is a very delectable warming sweet, plain as it may sound in the reading.

Your loving sister,

Hannah Woolley

The cat licked his paws and curled up into a ball beside the Aga as Melanie worked her way through the rest of the bundle. Each sheet of paper contained a hand-written recipe. Words that she could only guess at headed them. 'To make a March-pan' – *could it mean marzipan?* – 'To preserve Raspices' – *raspberries?* – and so on.

Melanie looked at her ruined Christmas pudding and pictured the smirk on her sister's face as she explained the calamity. She briefly contemplated a rescue mission – the pudding remnants would make a delicious festive-flavoured ice cream – but dismissed the idea as deeply unhygienic. She glared at the cat. "See the trouble you've caused, eh?"

She stepped over the pudding mess and surveyed her pantry. Half a packet of mince pies – 'finest' or not – would never keep them all happy. Sure, there were plenty of leftover currants and spices, but Christmas puddings took at least six weeks to mature. Starting from scratch at … she glanced at the clock on the wall … 3 a.m. on Christmas Day? Forget it. Then she spotted the packet of suet, wedged in between a jar of pickled walnuts and a bottle of rosemary-infused olive oil. She'd meant to throw the suet out after Stir-up Sunday but hadn't got around to it.

Wide-awake now, she looked at the bundle of recipes. Forgotten for centuries, it felt like fate that they had tumbled onto her floor amidst the pudding disaster.

73

"You're right, Cat, it would be nice to do an old-fashioned steamed pudding, even if it's not a proper Christmas pud."

With a mug of tea in one hand, she settled down to re-read them. There were three possibilities.

"Ollygog Pudding. Sounds like a heart attack-inducing golden syrup roly-poly. Can you imagine Pippa's face if I served that?" The cat squinted at her. "How about Uppey Pudding then? Hmm, maybe not. That's basically a mound of plain stodge. I could add a little cardamom …" She tried, and failed, to picture the kids eating cardamom, before pushing the recipe aside.

"OK, so our final entry for the emergency Christmas pudding competition is … Cat, you're supposed to provide a drum-roll here … or at least a purr of appreciation …" The cat flicked his tail. "I guess that'll do … our final contender is … Sussex Pond Pudding."   Glancing through the ingredients, Melanie decided this sounded luscious, oozing with sugary lemon juices, rather like the 'hidden orange' Christmas pudding that had sold out in every single supermarket around the country. Decision made, it didn't take her long to mix up the ingredients and pop it on the Aga to steam.

"Night, cat. Don't break anything else." She flicked the lights off.

The alarm went off at 7.30 a.m. Christmas morning had arrived. She pushed the patchwork quilt off and dragged herself out of bed. Optimistic as every kid in the country, she pulled the curtains back, hoping to see a magical white blanket of snow, but instead faced a gloomy grey drizzle.

With a sigh, she tugged them closed again. Downstairs, there was no sign of the cat and Melanie couldn't decide if she was pleased or disappointed. She'd kind of enjoyed chatting to it.

Years of catering college training came into play as she whizzed around the kitchen. She squashed the three-bird roast the local butcher had prepared into her roasting pan, took the nut loaf out of the fridge, adding the final flourish of dried cherries, sliced apricots and pecan nuts, then methodically tackled the side dishes. By the time she heard the excited chatter of her sugar-fuelled nephew and niece coming up the path, she was showered, dressed, and had even put some lipstick on.

"That smells amazing," Pippa gushed, air-kissing her cheeks. She glanced around.

"I love what you've done here. It could be out of a magazine."

Melanie scowled as Pippa fiddled with a garland then moved a cushion and a candle onto the stairs, before bribing Sarah into a ridiculously staged pose cradling a pine cone.

In his usual smart-casual uniform of a navy V-neck sweater, striped shirt and immaculately distressed jeans, Callum trailed in behind the others, laden with an assortment of identically- wrapped gifts decked out with over-sized tartan bows. He piled them under the tree before greeting his sister-in-law.

"Hi, Melanie, how's country life treating you?"

Prompt as ever, her mum arrived a few minutes later. Before she'd even got her coat off, the kids dragged everyone over to the tree. Melanie served small glasses of sherry (the only time of year she ever drank sherry, another family tradition) and mince pies, while the kids launched into a frenzy of present opening.

The family settled around the dining room table.

"Let me help you serve," Pippa said, leaping to her feet.

"I'm fine," Melanie replied. "If I can cater for 80, I'm pretty sure I can cope with six."

"Okay. Oh, look at these, they're so cute," Pippa said, snapping a pic of the gold and red beaded napkin rings that Melanie had woven. "Did you make them?"

Melanie carved the three-bird roast at the table, garnishing each plate with a dot of homemade cranberry jelly and a swirl of rich, thick gravy. Pippa interrupted the meal to take photos of every dish, sharing them with the world at regular intervals. Melanie grimaced as she rearranged the candles for each shot. *It's supposed to be about the food*, she thought.

Eventually, Melanie could put it off no longer; it was time for pudding. She'd been dreading this moment ever since they sat down. Plated up, it looked a little plain to her chef's eye. She sprinkled some edible gold leaf on the top and took a deep breath. Her entry to the dining room was greeted by a wall of horrified faces.

"But, Aunt Melanie, where's the Christmas Pudding?" Ben cried, as she placed the dish in the centre of the table.

"There was a little accident last night and it ended up on the kitchen floor."

Ben looked worried. "But what about our wishes? Will they still come true?"

"Oh, yes," Melanie reassured him, "I made sure they were safely inside this pudding for you, and the lucky coin too."

He and Sarah let out a collective sigh of relief and tucked into the pudding with relish.

"Ooh, it's actually rather yummy," her mum said. "So, what is it?"

"Sussex Pond Pudding."

Pippa wrinkled her nose. "It looks a bit funny. Did they teach you it at catering college?"

"Might as well have served Ollygog Pudding," Melanie muttered under her breath. "No. I found a pile of old recipes in the pantry and thought I'd try one." She showed her the bundle of letters.

"Vintage," Pippa squealed in delight, grabbing her phone for an Insta-opportunity. "Hannah Woolley. Have you googled her? Maybe she's famous."

"I doubt it," Melanie protested, but her sister was frantically tapping away on her phone.

"Look at this. She was published in 1672. Literally the first ever housekeeping blogger. Way before Mrs Beeton. People will love this … Hugh Feathering-what's-his-name will probably follow me …"

She took a snap of the recipes and started to type a post, her eyes sparkling, then suddenly she stopped.

"No, you should share this, Melanie. Food is your thing, not mine. Honestly, these recipes are amazing. You could start a blog … write a cookbook updating these for modern tastes." She glanced at the lake of sugary juices. "With a slightly healthier twist."

"But I don't know how to."

"I can show you, don't worry. It'll be our New Year project. We haven't done a project together since I made that hideous cotton wool ball snowman you insist on displaying every year!"

Melanie frowned, what was her sister playing at? "You remember making that?"

Before she had a chance to reply, Mum tottered back into the dining room carrying a tray of coffee and the obligatory tin of brightly-coloured, foil-wrapped chocolates. As Melanie got up to help with the coffee, the cat strolled in as if he owned the place. He wrapped himself around Melanie's legs, purring loudly.

Pippa reached over to stroke the cat.

"I didn't know you'd got a cat. How lovely, he'll be able to keep you company."

Irritated by the implication she might be lonely, Melanie forced the plunger down into the coffee, spurting grainy liquid over the tray.

"I haven't. He seems to have decided the pantry window is his personal cat flap." Her back turned, she missed Pippa snap a photo of her and upload it to her Insta feed.

#bestsisterever.

Lexi Rees

Lexi Rees, a Chindi author, grew up in the north of Scotland but now splits her time between London and West Sussex. She still goes back to Scotland regularly though. Usually seen clutching a mug of coffee and covered in straw and glitter, she spends as much time as possible sailing, horse riding, and crafting. She writes action-packed books for adventurous children and contemporary stories for grown-ups.

Christmas Repeats

by Phil Clinker

"On the first day of Christmas..."

Gwen sat on the bench on the prom, agitated and frustrated. She tutted loudly. She just couldn't get the song out of her head. And it was puzzling her. When, *exactly*, was the first day of Christmas? There were twelve of them, she knew. So, did it start twelve days before Christmas Day? That would have been the thirteenth. One day last week, she thought, but not with any conviction. Or would it be twelve days *from* Christmas Day? No, that didn't make sense. Nobody gives presents after Christmas Day, unless it's for a birthday. So the last present must have arrived on Christmas Day. Now, what did her true love give her...?

The Christmas lights on the lamp posts sparkled into her thoughts, and she looked on them with fondness for something she may have lost. If only she could remember.

"Excuse me, is this seat taken?"

Gwen emerged from her daydream with a start and looked round. She saw what she assumed was an elderly gentleman, thick woollen coat with collar turned up against the bitter wind, and wearing a rather jaunty peaked cap. She could not see his face, but a pair of blue twinkling eyes greeted her.

"Er, no, I don't think so," she mumbled, trying to get back to her song and her lights.

"Thank you," he said, sitting on the bench beside her. "The old legs are playing up, I'm afraid."

She didn't answer. She was thinking of the twelve lords a'leaping or whatever. And another thing, how did her true love wrap them all up?

"It's very bracing this morning, don't you think?"

Gwen turned once more to the man beside her. "Sorry?"

"The wind," he explained. "Bracing."

"Do I know you?" asked Grace, face scrunched up in confusion.

The man smiled. "No, but I can introduce myself if you'd like."

Gwen studied him for a second. "It's up to you," she said, noncommittally.

The man took off his cap with a theatrical flourish and waved it before her. "Gordon. The name's Gordon. Widower of this parish." His short tufts of grey hair flew in the wind, and he quickly replaced the cap. They sat in silence for a few moments, his eyes on the sea, her mind on maids a'milking. "Am I permitted to know your name?" he asked gently.

"Gwen," she said, then fell silent again.

A pair of gulls cawed loudly as they scrapped for scraps, and Gordon smiled at the scene. "It's beautiful here, don't you think?"

"What?" Gwen hadn't meant to be so abrupt, but she made no effort to apologise.

"I love it down here, on the prom. It's why we retired to Bognor," Gordon elaborated. "Me and Viv."

Gwen looked for this mysterious Viv.

"I lost her four years ago," said Gordon.

"Careless," said Gwen.

A car tooted noisily in the road below, and a group of lads pouring out of the pub jeered in a good-humoured mood. Gordon remembered days like that.

"Are you with anyone?" he said.

Gwen froze. *Was she with someone?* Well, for some reason she thought she ought to be, but for the life of her she couldn't be sure. She offered him a cross between a nod and a shrug.

"Well," said Gordon breezily, "I can sit with you until someone turns up. If that is all right?"

Gwen nodded this time. The old boy appeared harmless enough. She thought he looked smart, in a subdued way; nothing flashy — apart from the cap, of course. He had turned down the collar of his coat, so she could see a thin, long face, high cheekbones with a flash of crimson caused by the wind, and pursed lips under a white moustache. He started to smile.

They settled into a cosy stillness, only the sound of the waves and the wind breaking into their worlds. The promenade was fairly quiet, so close to Christmas, the holidaymakers opting for sunnier climes and more exotic locations. Gwen tried hard to think of places she might have visited, but without success. Not only that, but she'd forgotten where she had got to regarding the song, so she thought she might have to start again. It seemed to be happening more and more these days.

A youth on a skateboard raced by, mobile phone glued to his ear, and Gordon sighed. *What was the world coming to?* He pulled up the collar of his coat once more, feeling the chill of the late afternoon. Time was, he could have gone out without a shirt in this weather. Not any more. *Those that are left grow old.*

They sat together for half an hour, rarely speaking, but both feeling comfortable. Gordon offered her a boiled sweet, which she politely declined, and she asked him which was the first day of Christmas. He didn't know, either. Probably the thirteenth, he said, which she thought she had already decided, although she couldn't be sure.

Then, Gordon watched in astonishment as a woman rushed over and threw her arms around Gwen. "Mum, there you are!" she shrieked rather melodramatically, in Gordon's opinion. "We thought we'd lost you."

A man sidled up behind her, so obviously embarrassed by the tableau playing out in front of him. He tried to get the woman to hurry, but Gordon noticed with relish that Gwen was reluctant to leave the bench, and he gave her a silent cheer.

"She's fine," he said. "I've been keeping her company."

The woman gave him a sidelong glance. "Thank you," she said, without an ounce of gratitude. She helped Gwen to get up and adjusted her coat to make sure she was protected from the icy air. Then, with a haste which seemed obscene, to Gordon at least, they were gone.

"On the second day of Christmas…"

Gwen sat on the bench on the prom, agitated and frustrated. *No, no! That's not the song. It's the one with the boats… what is it?* It had come to her earlier, when she had left Melanie and that worthless husband of hers, whatever his name was, in the car park. She didn't need them. She was fine on her own. Had to be. Since Raymond went…

The Christmas lights sparkled on the lamp posts.

"Hello, Gwen."

She turned to see what appeared to be an elderly gentleman, thick woollen coat with collar turned up against the bitter wind, and wearing a rather jaunty peaked cap. His head was swathed in a green and white scarf, so she could see only his blue twinkling eyes.

"Do I know you?" asked Grace, face scrunched up in confusion.

He chuckled. "It's Gordon. We met yesterday, Gwen. Am I that easy to forget?"

She knew the answer to that question, but didn't want to upset him, whoever he was.

"Mind if I join you?" he asked, sitting beside her before she had a chance to reply. "Not so cold today, I think."

"If you say so."

Gordon studied the horizon. "I see no ships…"

"What?" Gwen hadn't meant to be so abrupt, but she made no effort to apologise.

"I couldn't help overhearing you. I think you were trying to remember the Christmas song about boats."

Gwen nodded. She hadn't realised she had been talking aloud. She ought to watch that in future.

"*I Saw Three Ships*," said Gordon.

"Yes," agreed Gwen. "Thank you."

Gordon settled onto the bench and crossed his long legs, despite the pain in his arthritic knees. He was determined to stay as active as possible, even if he suffered for it. "That was your daughter yesterday, I presume?" he said.

"Melanie, yes," Gwen confirmed with very little feeling. "And her husband," she added as a forlorn postscript.

Gordon shrugged. "Kids, eh? Real pain in the..." He stopped himself just in time. Gwen didn't seem to notice.

They sat mainly in silence, as they had the previous day, conversation not always necessary. The warmth of each other's company needed few words of expression. Two gulls, perhaps even the ones from yesterday, were padding along the prom, like a couple of sailors on the look-out for a good time, each one swaying with the movement of an imaginary ship. Gordon smiled.

"So, did you find Viv?" Gwen asked suddenly, causing him to choke back laughter.

"You remembered!" he exclaimed delightedly.

Gwen threw him a startled look. "Did I?" she said, then sank back. It hadn't occurred to her that she could remember anything.

"No, I'm afraid she's gone."

"Like my Raymond," Gwen said simply.

After a moment, Gordon said, "Do you live with your daughter?"

"No. They visit me most days at the home, take me out..."

"Lose you!" said Gordon mischievously. "Like yesterday."

Gwen grinned with childlike glee. "And today!"

Gordon slapped his leg. "Good on you, Gwen. I love a woman with passion!"

"Behave yourself!" she said reproachfully, pulling her coat closer round herself for protection.

Then, Gordon saw with a deepening gloom that Gwen's daughter was approaching. His brief moment of pleasure was over for another day. He liked Gwen, and could see the bonny young thing she had once been, still trying to escape. Life wasn't fair, but you just had to make the most of it.

Melanie shepherded her mother away from the bench without a backward glance, even as Gordon mumbled his goodbye. Then he stood, flexed his aching knees, and walked off in the opposite direction.

"On the third day of Christmas…"

Gwen sat on the bench on the prom, agitated and frustrated. She was fed up with it now. It wouldn't stop going round in her head. Everything had been fine when she could remember the songs and the words, but now it was all becoming a jumble. It was such terribly hard work, and she was getting tired.

The Christmas lights sparkled on the lamp posts.

"Hello, Gwen."

She turned to see what appeared to be an elderly gentleman, thick woollen coat with collar turned up against the bitter wind, and wearing a rather jaunty peaked cap. He had turned down the collar of his coat, so she could see a thin, long face, high cheekbones with a flash of crimson caused by the wind, and pursed lips under a white moustache. He started to smile, but all she focused on were his blue twinkling eyes.

"Do I know you?" asked Grace, face scrunched up in confusion.

Gordon perched on the bench beside her and gently placed his hand on hers. She did not flinch. "It's me, Gordon. From yesterday... and the day before. This is getting quite a habit." His eyes twinkled just a little bit more.

"Yes," she agreed, although she wasn't quite sure why.

"I've brought a flask of coffee," said Gordon, pulling it out of the carrier bag by his feet. "I hope you like coffee."

"Yes," she said, gratefully accepting the warmth of both the drink and the sentiment.

Gordon gave her a conspiratorial wink. "I've put a little something in it, Gwen. Well, it is Christmas!"

Gwen shivered with the excitement of it all.

"Cheers!" toasted Gordon.

"Cheers!" echoed Gwen, and they both burst into a fit of the giggles, while clinking their plastic cups together.

"Only five days to the Big One, then," observed Gordon ruefully. "I suppose you'll be having a big knees-up at the home."

"I suppose," Gwen said.

"I've got my son and family down for a couple of days. Keeps me on my toes," said Gordon. He hesitated. "Perhaps I'll see you in the New Year?"

"Yes," said Gwen, not too sure whether that was the right answer to give him, but feeling that it probably was.

They sat together, like Darby and Joan, for very nearly an hour, before Melanie caught up with them. Gordon wondered if it had been a deliberate ploy, allowing the old folk to enjoy some time together – or whether it was just a case of letting someone else look after her mother for a while. Either way, Gordon was very happy.

As Melanie fussed over her mother, she slipped a card into Gordon's hand and gave him an awkward smile. Gordon nodded his thanks and turned away, picking up his carrier bag.

"What did you say your name was again?" Gwen's voice trailed over his shoulder, and a deep sadness engulfed him.

"So here it is, merry Christmas, everybody's having fun…"

Slade's massive number one boomed through the hall as Gordon took a tentative step inside. It was three days to Christmas, and his son was arriving tomorrow; but here he was, dressed up to the nines and ready to party. The hall looked amazing. The food looked amazing. Gwen looked amazing, off into the distance. So different to how she had looked on the prom.

The Christmas lights sparkled on the huge tree.

Gordon was approached by a middle-aged woman wearing a pale blue uniform and apron, who looked questioningly at him. He produced from his pocket the invitation Melanie had given him, and the woman waved him in with a wide smile.

Gwen turned to see what appeared to be an elderly gentleman, sporting a nicely tailored suit and a green and white striped tie. She could clearly see a thin, long face, high cheekbones with a flash of crimson caused by the heat in the room, and pursed lips under a white moustache. But all she focused on were his blue twinkling eyes. "Hello, Gordon," she said; and then, with the most radiant of smiles, she added, "I remembered!"

Gordon grinned like the Cheshire Cat. It was going to be a most wonderful Christmas.

Phil Clinker

When he retired three years ago, Phil took up painting and also returned to his first love – writing. 2019 has been a special year for him: in April he was shortlisted for the Bognor Regis Write Short Story Competition; at the end of May his debut novel, *Bakerton*, was published by Pegasus Publishing, who also asked for first refusal on his next two books; and then came the selection of *Christmas Repeats* for this anthology. He lives in Bognor with his wife, Olive, and is currently halfway through his second novel, *Thurlow Junction*, which once again features the unconventional Sheriff John Withers.

Stranger on the Shore

by Angela Petch

"We'll zip you up nice and warm, it's really cold out there today, Jamie."

Mary pulled on her little son's snow suit and gently fed his fingers into his red gloves.

"Make a starfish with your fingers. Let's try not to get two in one this time."

They always played the glove game when they were getting ready to go out, just like her mother had when Mary was young. When she was a teenager, she'd been determined to do her own thing with any children she might have one day, and yet now she sounded just like her mother. Continuing these routines was a way of keeping her close, now she wasn't around. Mary tried not to be angry that her mother hadn't seen Kitty's first tooth, witnessed her late walking or her first appearance in the nativity play. Jamie was born six months after his grandmother lost her battle with cancer. Mary tried not to be bitter out of respect for her mother's gentle nature. But it was hard.

"Can I push Jamie today? You promised." Her daughter's plaintive request interrupted her memories.

"If you're good and if Sammy doesn't pull too much, then I'm sure you can, Kitty."

The walk from their cottage at Selsey towards Pagham Harbour was only a brisk ten-minute hike if you were on your own, but Mary's straggly procession made it more of a dawdle. She had to manage a push chair with Jamie cocooned inside his fleecy blankets, whilst controlling Sammy the pointer, who was desperate to be off the leash to explore the mud flats. All the while she had to keep an eye on six-year-old Kitty who was determined to crush the ice on every puddle between the village and the marsh.

It was good to be out in the fresh air, despite the December cold. Last week's snow still hung around, frozen in the ditches. At home, she'd have had a battle with Kitty over switching on the television, full of the pre-Christmas frenzy, including lots of adverts hawking the latest, expensive, must-have toys.

They passed the tiny stone memorial to Kitty Childs that Mary's own Kitty claimed was hers. The tide was out. The haunting cries of little terns and sandpipers carried across the muddy expanse and the tang of seaweed was strong in the wind as the little band made its way along the shingle path, stepping over lacy lines of shells and black seaweed tossed up by the morning tide.

Just before their special spot at Church Norton, they diverted up a path towards the tiny, historic chapel of St Wilfrid to look at the remains of the Norman castle nearby. Mary helped Kitty read the words on the sign, describing what the mound of grass had looked like many years ago, but the little girl was full of whys and didn't seem to understand how the place had once been busy, brimming with soldiers making ready for battle.

Their next destination was a group of oaks that grew horizontally from the bank, their thick branches convoluted from the effects of sea and wind. Kitty loved to climb and conquer them. The mud here was perfect for building castles and Mary pulled out a couple of spades from beneath the pram to hand to the children. She sat on one of the trees, its branches snaking along the shore like a whalebone carcass, and watched her little family. If she was lucky, she could sometimes snatch precious moments to read a couple of pages of her library book. Today, she simply gazed at gulls in the distance, as they fluttered and swooped over the sea, like dozens of hankies tossed in the wind.

She was peeved when she saw an old man sitting on one of the oaks. Naturally, the area belonged to everybody, but she was used to claiming these trees for her family. He looked harmless enough, but you could never be sure nowadays with some of the awful news in the papers. She'd warned Kitty already of the danger of talking to strangers. Unstrapping Jamie from his push chair, she moved her camp as far away from the man as she could. He hardly seemed to notice their arrival, sitting hunched up, staring out over the marshes. He was hatless and his hands were thrust deep in the pockets of his thin waterproof.

Although he looked cold and lonely, and might have enjoyed their company, Mary kept her distance. Jamie hunkered down to dig in the shell-strewn mud with his yellow spade and Kitty filled her pail and emptied its contents to start the foundations of their castle. Near the eroding bank Mary found a scattering of gull feathers, probably the result of a fox's breakfast, and she collected them to take home to make a Red Indian head dress. For a long as she could, she intended to encourage her children into games of invention and imagination, just as her own mother had done. They'd never had the money to splash out on expensive toys because Dad had died very young. But Mum had filled their childhood with fun.

Mary and her brothers would build tents in their strip of back garden by slinging sheets over the washing line. They'd put on plays and strut about in the kitchen in dresses and scarves plundered from their mother's wardrobe. The scrubbed pine table was turned upside down to become a pirate's ship. It didn't matter if water splashed everywhere when they turned the sink into a sea to sail boats modelled from plastic containers, engaged in fierce battle. Mary thought there was too much obsession with neatness and minimalism. Some of her friends' children were only allowed to make a mess during the village hall play group sessions, and never at home.

Jamie's crying brought her back to the present day. He'd pitched nose first into Kitty's battlements. The old man had rushed to help him before Mary could reach him, and with clumsy hands was brushing sand and tears from Jamie's crab-apple cheeks.

"Thank you – I'll take over," she said, scooping her baby into her arms and taking him back to the fallen tree.

"There, Mummy's here, let me have a look."

"You should've been watching him," the old man scolded. "He could have fallen in the water."

"Yes, well, you need eyes in the back of your head with this little chap."

Who did he think he was, talking to her like that?

She turned away from the old man, rocking her little son in her arms and soothing him with kisses until his screaming stopped. "There, it's nothing, my little sausage.

All over now. We'll clean you up properly once we're home."

Jamie struggled to be out of his mother's arms, impatient to get back to the fun of busily doing nothing in the mud, moving piles of stones and shells from one side to the other.

"There's all kinds of hidden dangers here on the shore," continued the man, "you should take nothing for granted."

She ignored him. He was obviously a weirdo and she was annoyed he'd spoiled the afternoon and invaded their space.

"Come on, Kitty, we're going. Put the bucket and spades back under the buggy."

"Oh Mum, do we have to? We've only just got here. Don't be a spoilsport."

But her mind was made up.

Back home she helped Kitty make gingerbread shapes to hang on the Christmas tree and ignored the flour and sugar treading into the floor. It was her way of making up to the children.

The old man was near the shingle path again, two days later. Mary had thought about him in the intervening days and decided she'd previously been rude and abrupt. This time, when Kitty wandered up to him, she watched cautiously but didn't stop her daughter.

"Are you Father Christmas?" she heard her daughter ask.

"I wouldn't be sitting here if I was, would I, little miss? I'd be too busy making last-minute toys," he replied gruffly.

"You look like Father Christmas with your long white whiskers."

The old man put a hand to his bushy sideburns and smiled.

"Kitty, don't be rude. Come and play over here!" Mary called.

"She's all right. Leave her be."

Kitty continued to talk to the old man as she shovelled mud into her bucket. He bent down next to the little girl and gently supervised.

"What you need for that fine castle is a drawbridge to pull up when the enemy attacks. I'll find you a good piece of wood."

The old man wandered off and fetched driftwood from just below the tide mark.

Kitty pointed to a stump of wood embedded in the sand.

"You could've chopped a bit off that."

"Oh no, that wouldn't do. That's a bit of history that is. It's the remains of an old berth."

"Like when babies are born? Like baby Jesus at Christmas?"

He chuckled, "Not that kind. It sounds the same. No, this kind of berth has most likely been here for hundreds of years. It probably dates from when Pagham was an important harbour and big vessels traded wool to Europe. Imagine lots of boats moored here in these waters."

He straightened up and gazed into the distance, shielding his eyes with one hand. "I reckon this place was far more important in them days than London."

"That's where Daddy works," the little girl said. "He goes to London by train each day, but not by boat. He gets home after I've gone to bed, and he hasn't had time to build my doll's house for Christmas. Are you going to get lots of presents from your family?"

"Let's get this castle built before the tide comes in again,' the old man said, kneeling down to dig with the children, ignoring her question.

Mary joined in and between them they constructed the best castle ever, with a moat, a drawbridge, flagged turrets, all made from flotsam and jetsam washed up onto the marsh.

"That was fun. I'm sorry if we disturbed your peace. I'm Mary by the way,' she said. She extended a sandy, mittened hand to the old man. He didn't take it but smiled back kindly.

"I'm Stan. Stan Harper from Holly Cottage. Haven't built a castle in years. You've got a fine family here, young lady. Be sure you look after them carefully."

Later that evening, Mary sat by the fire enjoying her quiet hour; the time of calm after she had bathed the children and settled them to bed, while she waited for Rob to return from his slog of a commute from London. During the week he had to leave for work at six a.m. and he usually arrived home after eight o'clock, if he was lucky. She regretted how he had ended up on this treadmill. At weekends he was so jaded, and they were doing less and less together as a family. They'd been arguing lots lately over stupid things and she had to keep reminding herself he was tired and to make allowances for his grouchiness. But she feared they were drifting apart. The sparkle was seeping away from their marriage.

There was a knock at the door. To her surprise it was Stan Harper, with a large cardboard box in his arms. "I hope you won't be offended Mary, but I thought maybe this would do for young Kitty."

"Come in, come in. Don't stand out there in the cold."

She led him into the warm living-room.

"You've got it looking nice," he said, glancing at the easy chairs by the hearth and the tree in the corner, heavy with festive decorations.

"It was practically derelict when we moved in," she said.

"I remember it well."

He took a doll's house from the carton. It was modelled on a Victorian house, with three storeys and furniture from that period. In the kitchen was an old-fashioned mangle, a tiny blacked range and a set of miniature bells on the wall to summon the maids. She peered at the details.

"It's absolutely beautiful, Stan. But far too generous a gift."

"There's no point in hanging onto it. It's been in this box for years. Please take it, Mary. Enjoy it with your family."

An idea popped into her brain. "What are you doing on Christmas day?" she asked. "Would you come and share lunch with us? It'll just be the four of us, mind, and nothing too grand. The children don't have any grandparents and Kitty would love a grandfather for Christmas."

Stan came on Christmas day and he and Rob sat near the hearth after lunch with glasses of brandy while Jamie slept, curled up in Stan's lap. It was fascinating to hear him recount old stories about the village in his soothing burr of a voice; he told them about the local Mulberry Harbour project during the Second World War — preparation for top-secret Operation Overlord and the invasion of Normandy.

"And once upon a time," he continued, "there were windmills all over the joint. The harbour used to work well, especially in the eighteenth century, but it's all choked with weeds and silt now. I've heard tell about smugglers decoying revenue officers from Sidlesham, while rafts of tubs were landed at Pagham from a galley out at sea. Oh yes, there's lots about this place we will probably never know."

Kitty sat and played with her doll's house and Mary, watching the scene from the doorway to the kitchen, thought it looked like an old-fashioned Christmas card. The log fire glowed and the Christmas tree, scraping the beams of the cosy living room, was laden with painted fir cones and home-made biscuits. She fetched her camera to capture the memory on film.

After New Year, when Kitty was back at school, Mary took their thank-you letters to the post office in Pagham Road. There was one for Stan from Kitty, but she needed the full address before she could post it. Sheila, the postmistress, frowned when Mary asked where Holly Cottage was.

"I'm not sure, my dear. Just wait while I check with Ollie."

The post office was in the corner of the store and Ollie came from behind the counter where he'd been slicing bacon.

"It's where you live, Mary. Your cottage used to be known as Holly Cottage."

"But ours is Rose Cottage. That's partly why we gave Kitty her middle name. I'm looking for Stan Harper. He's quite old. Maybe he's a little confused."

Ollie and Sheila looked at each other.

"Stan Harper, the carpenter? He died more than twenty years ago," said Ollie, and Sheila continued, "in a sailing accident on the river. The whole family drowned. It was dreadful. There was a storm; their boat went down, and their bodies weren't found for weeks."

"In fact, Stan's body was never washed up, was it, Sheila? A lot of us men were involved in the search, but he was never found, poor old soul."

The post was waiting on the door mat when Mary arrived home, including an envelope with the Christmas photos she'd sent off to be developed. Without taking her coat off or removing Jamie from his pushchair, she ripped it open to search for her Christmas card scene. Sheila and Ollie were surely wrong. Stan had been in their own home, eating roast turkey and pulling crackers as real as the tree standing in the corner, which had to come down today. She leafed through the pages until she found the fireside scene. The image was a little blurred, but she made out Rob in one armchair and Kitty on the carpet at his feet next to the doll's house. The shape of Jamie was indistinct. He was bundled up asleep on the opposite chair, but his outline was very fuzzy. Of Stan there was not a single trace.

Mary left the children alone with Rob on Saturday afternoon and took Sammy on his lead for a walk along the coastal path. As she approached the tree, she wondered if the old man would be there again. But he wasn't, and she lingered for a while, throwing sticks for Sammy. Eventually, when she understood that Stan wasn't coming, she took the thank-you letter from her pocket and stuffed it down a hole in the trunk.

"I promise to take great care of my family," she shouted, and the wind carried her words over the marshes and mingled with the honks from the Brent geese nearer the shore.

And family means all of us, starting with Rob, she said inside her head. We need him with us. I'm going to do my best to persuade him to find a job nearer home. We'll start again; we'll make it work.

She whistled for Sammy and as they started back for home, she thought she caught a movement in the reed beds, but it was most likely shadows cast by the wintry sun peeping from behind scudding clouds; a trick of the light. Pulling her bobble hat further down over her curls, she hurried back to her family, leaving the marsh to settle in the dying sun.

Angela Petch

Angela Petch, a Chindi author, shares her year between the remote Tuscan Apennines and the Sussex seaside. Born in Germany, she spent six years as a child in Rome, worked in Amsterdam after finishing her Italian degree, moved to Sicily for her job with a Dutch construction company, then on to Tanzania for three years. Her head is full of stories and pen and notebook accompany her on all her travels.

She is the author of two multi-layered historical novels set in Italy, including an emotional, Amazon best-selling WW2 story, *The Tuscan Secret*, published in 2019 by Bookouture. A sequel will appear in 2020.

In 2018, in memory of her best friend, she self-published *Mavis and Dot*, a gently humorous novella located by the Sussex seaside. It was awarded a Five Star Award from One Stop Fiction. All profits go to cancer research.

Her short stories appear in The People's Friend and PRIMA.

The Best-Behaved Girl in Bognor

by Julia Macfarlane

All I wanted for Christmas was a china doll. All I had ever wanted, for as far back as I could remember, was a china doll; and I was eight that year so I had quite a few disappointed Christmases behind me. I had Bessie, my rag doll, who wore miniature replicas of my dresses, all made with love by Mummy, including of course, Bessie herself, with her calico cotton arms and legs and artfully embroidered face. But oh, to have a china doll!

I had already determined that I would try again this Christmas. In my best handwriting, I would place 'A China Doll' at the top of my list to Father Christmas, and as my letter's edges blackened and curled in their flight up the chimney to his home in Lapland, I would also pray to the Baby Jesus to hear my prayer.

I had told nobody my plan yet because last year Mummy had told me that Father Christmas could only carry a few china dolls in his sleigh 'to avoid breakages', as if they were eggs, and that only the really good little girls would receive them. And Daddy had said, "Only the good little girls with rich daddies, I've heard." Mummy had shushed him and Daddy's moustaches had twitched in a way that told me it was one of his jokes that was not really funny. I knew they were both wrong because Violet Daughtrey had three china dolls squashed into her Silver Cross doll's pram, and Mummy said she was a very wicked little girl who left her bedroom in a terrible mess, according to the maids who worked there; and their cook said Mr Daughtrey was in hock to all the tradesmen to the extent that she was ashamed to look them in the eye when they called.

Today was a Saturday and I should have been dressed in my play clothes and chased out of the house along with Ronald and Dennis. Instead we were all decked out in our Sunday best, including poor Daddy who ran his finger under his shirt collar and complained about the fuss. "We are only walking three streets into town. You'd think we were going to a wedding!"

"Shush, dear." Mummy said. "If Mr Meek has been kind enough to offer you a discount for work well done, I don't want him thinking your family are a pack of ragamuffins. Ronald, kick your brother one more time and you shall feel my hand, young man!"

Mr Meek owned Meek's Haberdashery on London Road. On the first floor of the shop, he kept his more expensive items, and ladies were invited up to view the costlier rolls of cloth and household goods. I had never been up those stairs, and nor had Mummy, but Daddy had won the contract to renovate the shop with new shelves and work surfaces. Mr Meek had been so pleased with the results that he had invited my daddy to 'bring his lady wife in to purchase a few items from the first floor at discount'.

Daddy said, "He's no fool, mind, Ethel. Offering me discount as he hands me my wage – what better way to make sure the money goes straight back into his pocket!"

Mummy had been too excited to care and even more so when Daddy gave her a white £5 note to spend! She had hugged him close and said over his shoulder to me: "Watch me turn this five into twenty, eh, Maisie? You'll help me, won't you?"

I had nodded, my piece of bread and dripping halfway to my mouth. Mummy was very good at making things to sell. We painted wooden boxes and stuck shells all over them to sell to the tourists in the summer; Mummy took in sewing jobs, and made patchwork quilts and clippie mats from the remnants. Daddy sent the boys crabbing to sell to the hotels and pubs, and of course everyone knew Daddy was the best carpenter in Bognor.

Eventually we were ready and made it into town without mishap. On the way to Mr Meek's we passed Toyland in the Arcade and I stopped short at the sight of the window display. There in the centre was *my china doll!* She was just as I had imagined her: real hair ringlets the colour of spun gold, tied up with a thin ribbon, the colour of a Bognor summer sky. She had long eyelashes on eyelids that would close when laid to rest, and her rosy lips and cheeks were painted onto perfect, creamy skin. She wore a dress of ivory lace edged with more blue ribbon and on her feet were the neatest, pale kid, lace-up shoes. "Sylvia!" I breathed, because I had always known her name would be Sylvia, and flattened my face against the window the better to take her in.

Mummy pulled at my arm. "Don't you dare lick that window!" she hissed, then saw what I was looking at. "Aah, not a china doll again, Maisie. "

And Daddy said, "I don't think the child exists that is good enough to deserve that wee beauty!"

I scowled at them both. "I am going to be that girl!" I announced. "You shall see!" And I waved goodbye to my beautiful china doll who stared past me up to the wrought iron ceiling, placed my hand dutifully into Mummy's and prepared to walk on, the best-behaved child in Bognor.

At Mr Meek's we were met inside the door by Colin, a nervous young man, who bowed us in and invited Mummy to: "Please to step upstairs, Mr Meek is expecting you." Head held high, Mummy sailed past her few acquaintants on the ground floor and up the wooden staircase with the rest of us trailing behind her.

Mr Meek came out from behind a polished wood and glass display counter to shake my parents' hands. Had he then escorted her back downstairs again without a penny being spent, it would still have been one of the happiest days in her life.

"What a lovely family you have!" Mr Meek commented as he bowed over her outstretched, gloved hand. "Such a skilled man as Mr Tuppen deserves no less, and I am delighted to make your acquaintance."

"Charmed, I'm sure," she replied. I sat myself on one of the wooden chairs against a wall and rested my hands in my lap, determined to be the most angelic child in existence. Daddy jerked his head at my brothers to do the same. Mr Meek was showing Mummy some rolls of thick, dark worsted but Mummy shook her head.

"If you don't mind, Mr Meek, I have in mind some good quality flannel – like those over there." And she moved across to another counter. Mr Meek swallowed and followed her.

"These are rather expensive, Mrs Tuppen," he tried but Mummy merely smiled.

"I know that, Mr Meek, but you are offering a discount." She fingered a cherry red cloth. "This and the grey, I think, please. And I need some broderie anglaise and some thick crocheting wool for the borders, but I expect I can buy those downstairs – still with the discount, I hope?" And she smiled her most radiant smile at him. "Now, how many yards of each do you think I could purchase for - let's say three guineas?"

I heard Daddy, who had lounged against the wall next to me, give a low groan. "I think you are about to find out, Mr Meek, what a hard-headed businesswoman my wife is. She comes from up North, you see."

Mummy gave him one of her looks. "My parents ran a small dairy near Crawley, Mr Meek. My husband may be referring to the fact that I helped out on market days."

"May I say, madam, intelligence and beauty combined is a rarity to be admired and envied." And he bowed low again. Ronald and Dennis snorted into their handkerchiefs and I began to think Mr Meek was a bit of a creep. He measured out the two cloths against the brass ruler inlaid into the wooden counter. The cherry had only a few twirls left on its cardboard roller when he had finished. He was about to cut and replace the tube when he caught my mother's eye. With a tight little grimace, as if he had felt a twinge in his appendix, he muttered: "Perhaps I can throw this last piece in as a goodwill gesture." Mummy inclined her head in thanks and Daddy gave a one-note chuckle and shook his head   in a way that suggested he was secretly tickled pink by her antics.

"May I enquire as to the plans you have for this material, Mrs Tuppen?"

107

"Clothes for the boys," she gestured towards the grey. "New pinafore for Maisie, skirt and jacket for me," she gestured to the red. "And with what is left, I shall make some hearthrugs to sell to the bigger houses."

Mr Meek stroked his goatee beard. "Would you consider selling them to me, Mrs Tuppen? I would give you a good price, say 30% commission to me for each one sold at your usual price."

Mummy glanced at Daddy who gave a small nod. "Make it 20%, Mr Meek, and you have a deal." She held out her hand in a very business-like manner to seal the deal. Daddy gave another low-level chuckling groan.

Business done, Mr Meek offered to send the goods to our home, which Mummy graciously accepted as if that were quite normal for our family purchases. I suspect, and so did Daddy, that Mr Meek didn't want his other customers to see how much Mummy had bought 'at a discount'.

That night, Daddy suggested we should think about our letters to Father Christmas. I had finished mine while Ronald was still sucking his pencil, trying to decide between a catapult and a bow and arrow, and Dennis was having 't-r-a-i-n s-e-t' spelled out to him letter by letter, as he painfully drew the lopsided letters. I tried to put mine on the fire before Mummy and Daddy could read it. I did not want them refusing my wish before Father Christmas even got a chance to see it. But Daddy was too quick for me. "Got to check the spelling, Maisie!" He grinned at Mummy and she grinned back. Why checking my spelling should be something that makes them happy I will never understand?   Plus, Daddy knows I am one of the best spellers in the class.

There were several items on my list: The china doll from the window of Toyland; sweets for my brothers and me; a pretty brooch for Mummy; a fat cigar with a gold band for Daddy.

Daddy read it through and passed it to Mummy without comment, which was worrying. She put Dennis down from her lap and took the sheet. She tightened her lips as she read it, then pinched the top of her nose between her fingers. Her eyes glistened in the firelight

"A china doll again, Maisie? Are you sure? In a year or two you'll be too big for dolls."

"I won't! And even if I am, Mummy, I shall keep her safe for my little girls when I grow up. And I will have two years to love her and play with her if I get her this year, so this is the year…"

"Enough!" said Daddy. He sounded cross but then he smiled at me.   "We can't promise anything, little one. China dolls are very expensive and very fragile. You would have to keep it safe from this pair of heathens." He ruffled their heads. "Are you sure there is nothing else that you would rather have?"   He pulled me onto his knee and cupped my chin in his dry, rough hand. I shook my head and looked earnestly into his blue eyes.

"She is all I want, and I promise I will look after her. She will be a sister to Bessie. And I know china dolls are only for good little girls – but you shall see! I will do every job you ask me between now and Christmas Day. I will feed the chickens, I will help in the kitchen…"

Daddy stopped me with a finger on my lips. "Ssh! It's alright. Your letter is perfect and I will send it up the chimney myself." He looked at Mummy over my head and she looked back, giving a tiny nod. My letter was placed on the fire and I watched it twist and curl before its ashes went up the chimney flue with the smoke and sparks. I was the happiest girl in Bognor.

I was as good as my word. I set to every chore with a smile on my face. As Mummy finished the hearth rugs, she rolled them up carefully, tied them with a piece of clean white sacking, and twice a week or more, I trundled my little wooden pram to Mr Meek's – the tradesmen's entrance – and handed over the goods. In return I received a little brown envelope to be carefully taken home. More material arrived in the house and Mummy looked pale and tired, her hands even redder than usual, as she worked hard late into every evening, fulfilling the orders and working on mysterious preparations for Christmas after we had gone to bed. And every time I visited the town centre, I slipped into the Arcade to gaze at my beautiful doll.

A week before Christmas, as I reached Toyland's window, Mrs Daughtrey was leaving the shop. I overheard her say to the assistant inside. "And somebody has already bought the doll, you say? Then why leave it in the window, for goodness sake!" And she banged the door to. Oh, Sylvia, my Sylvia! I thought my heart would break. I barged into the shop and cried out to the young girl behind the counter. "Who has bought the doll? Please can you tell me, please, miss!"

"Maisie, isn't it?" said the girl. "I can't say who has bought it, love, but it will be disappearing off to Lapland very soon. Or how else will Father Christmas be able to deliver it?" And she smiled at me, as if I was a much smaller and stupider child than I am.

Back home, Mummy cuddled me when she saw my tears and said, "Where there's life there's hope." When Daddy came home, he offered to carve me a huge wooden doll on Christmas Day, if I was still disappointed with my gifts. And I felt they were secretly laughing at me, so I forgot about being an angel and went to bed early in an outraged huff.

Christmas Eve arrived at last. Sleep seemed impossible. I spent the night in a torment of wakefulness and yet, somehow, I awoke in the dark twilight of a cold Christmas morning to the shrieks of excitement coming from my brothers' bedroom. The air was icy outside my thick eiderdown and I lay in a fever of anticipation and dread. Was my Sylvia here or had some other little girl been given her? I lifted my head and looked towards the foot of my bed. Daddy's red woollen sock was visible in the grey light, and as my eyes adjusted, I could see that it bulged with goodies. Letting the cold sneak between my sheets, I raised myself on one elbow, so as to see better what other treasures were there. A doll's dress was draped over the wooden rail. I recognised the red flannel, cut from the same cloth as the new pinafore I had worn to the Christmas service yesterday evening. A new dress for Bessie. Oh, please, does that mean there is no new doll – had all my hard work been in vain? But, as my eyes adjusted to the low light, I saw   a new wooden crib by the window and golden hair resting on the pillow.

She was here, my Sylvia was here!

She was mine, she was mine!

Ignoring the cold on my feet, I knelt down and cradled her in my arms – my own beautiful baby. Her eyes were dutifully closed in sleep but as I lifted her to examine her dainty clothes, she opened them and we looked for the first time into each other's eyes. I could not wait to show the rest of the family. Holding her tight, I opened my bedroom door.

A new clippy mat lay on the landing – made from the red and grey flannel scraps, exquisitely made by Mummy - a gift to the house for Christmas Day. My bare feet tripped on it and as I fell full-length, Sylvia flew from my hands. She performed a perfect gymnastic arc, displaying her silk and lace-trimmed bloomers to perfection before her head crashed against the wall at the turn of the stairs. As she somersaulted downwards, she left shards of broken bisque on every tread she hit.

Julia Macfarlane

Julia Macfarlane is a Durham lass who followed her daughter to West Sussex when she fell in love with a Bognor boy while at Manchester University. Julia 'retired' from University senior management but now runs Aldwick Publishing, Bognor Regis Write Club and is Programme Secretary for the Bognor Regis & District Ramblers, as well as being an active and enthusiastic member of the Charles Dickens Fellowship Portsmouth.

A collection of her short stories has been published as *News of Leon & Other Tales.*

Julia has also produced anthologies of stories and poems with fellow Sussex writers: *A Blast On The Waverley's Whistle;* and *The View From Here'* and is co-editor of this book.

She has compiled the popular *Chichester Ghost Tour,* and leads bemused tourists around Chichester on her entertaining private tours.

These can be booked via bognorwriters@gmail.com.

Find out more at her website:
www.macfarlanejuliawriter.com.

Winter Solstice
by Patricia Osborne

Uncle Geoff runs towards us as we pull up outside St Nicholas' Church. Dad winds down the window. "What's the problem?"

"He's not here yet," Uncle Geoff pants. "Maybe go around the block for a bit?"

Dad tuts. "Where is he?" Dad taps the driver. "Drive around for a few minutes, please, mate." He turns to me. "I knew that lazy lout would let you down."

"Don't start, Dad."

"But, Megan, we just want the best for you. Girls don't have to get married so young these days. It's not like in the seventies when I married your mum. You have the chance to go to university."

"I don't want to go to university. I want to marry Alex. And just because he wears a leather jacket doesn't make him a lout or lazy. If you took the time to get to know him you'd see that he's gentle and kind. He won't let me down."

The chauffeur starts up the car. Dad sits grunting as we circle roads with Christmas lights across house windows. One house has an inflatable Santa bobbing on its porch roof. I'd be Mrs Chambers by Christmas Day. The best present in the world. We drive under a bridge by Three Bridges Station before making our way back to the church where the white limousine comes to a halt. Dad steps out of the car, helps me out, lifts my long train and we stroll up the path to the church, stopping in the porch.

Lou, my best friend, looks gorgeous in her burgundy bridesmaid dress. She hugs me. "You look amazing. That gown is perfect on you."

I shiver. "Thanks. It's difficult to sit down in with its huge skirt and net petticoats. Anyway, never mind that. Is Alex here yet?"

"No, but don't worry, Ben's not here either but they will be. Relax." Lou puts her arm around me.

Dad paces up and down. "He'd better turn up, that's all I can say. Messing my daughter around. Irresponsible lout."

"Don't, Dad." I lift my bouquet to hide my expression. The winter flowers make me sneeze.

The first day I'd met Alex, he'd swaggered towards me. His black leather jacket was unzipped and his scarf had come loose, showing a part-fastened shirt and a gold chain around his neck. Butterflies fluttered in my stomach. Of course it must've been Lou he was after, with her big boobs and long blonde hair, not mousy little me with the flat chest. She looked so grown up. It didn't help that Mum never let me wear make-up. "You're only sixteen, Megan. Plenty of time for that."

"Hiya," he said, "what are you lovely babes doing down in Brighton? Do you live here?"

"No," I answered, "we've come to see the Christmas lights."

"How about you lot?" Lou signalled to the gang of bikers.

"Been to a rally. I bet you've seen a lot of us around today. That's my chopper over there." He pointed to a long-bodied motorbike with stretched handlebars. "I'm Alex." He looked at me.

"Megan."

"Where've you been hiding all my life, Megan?" He smiled.

His smile sent those butterflies racing in my stomach.

No. Alex won't let me down. I just know it. I look around me. The Church notice board is advertising the Christingle Service for this Sunday. Green foliage wreaths with huge red bows hang down from the arched leaded windows.

Mum nudges me. She's come out of the church. "Are you listening to me, Megan? I said, we need to get you home. He's not coming. I knew we shouldn't have let you go ahead with this farce."

"He'll be here. Something must have happened to delay him."

The vicar joins us. "Have you heard anything? It's getting very late."

"He'll be here," I say, again. "Please can you wait a bit longer?"

The vicar glances at his watch and sighs. "Fine. Fifteen minutes. I've a funeral at three."

A motorcycle with a pink sidecar, decorated in gold tinsel, roars up. Ben climbs off the bike and runs up the church path. "Megan, you've got to come. It's Alex."

"What's happened?" I ask.

"Just come. You too, Lou."

Struggling in high heels, I lift up my train, and follow Ben to the bike.

"What? Where the hell do you think you're going with my daughter?" Dad tries to chase but his extra weight makes him waddle.

Ben grabs the bouquet out of my hands and chucks it on the grass verge. "You won't be needing that. Get in." He points to my carriage. "Wrap that blanket around yourself."

I hoist up my gown, climb inside the sidecar, squishing the dress fabric down, and put the crash helmet on just as Dad reaches us. He picks up my expensive bouquet and shouts, "Megan." He makes for his car but can't get through, as the gang of bikers have formed a blockade.

"Lou, quick. On the back." Ben raises his voice to be heard above the engine.

"I'm calling the Police. Kidnapping my daughter." Dad gets out his mobile.

Ben revs the bike and we spin off. I've no idea what's happening. Ben looks frantic. Something's happened to Alex. If only Mum and Dad had let us get married earlier. We'd have had more time. Why did we have to wait until I was eighteen? I knew this wedding dress was going to be a curse, but Lou talked me into handing over fifty pounds to the bereaved bride.

"It's not really second-hand," the girl said, with tears in her eyes, "I never got a chance to wear it. My fiancé was killed in a car crash, but you look lovely in it." Was the same thing happening again, now, with Alex?

Ben speeds along the main road with a convoy of bikers behind. My bare arms and face are freezing without a coat or scarf. Goodness knows what state my dress will be in once I get out of here. I try to snuggle

117

under the wool blanket but it's difficult as I'm rocked backwards and forwards. Ben takes the corner, the sidecar feels like it's off the ground. I scream. At this rate, I'm not going to get out alive. After what seems forever, Ben finally pulls into Holystead Woods, just the other side of Horsham, and stops.

"We're here," he says smiling.

"Thank God for that." I sigh with relief and clamber out, almost tripping up on my dress. "Is Alex alright? Where is he?"

"He's fine. Don't worry. Never mind Alex for now. You need to get changed. Shannon," he calls.

Shannon rushes over. "Come on." She takes my hand, smiling, and drags me across to a barn that's radiating heat. Lou follows behind.

Shannon points to my gown. "Let's get that off and put this one on instead." She holds out a cream cheesecloth dress.

I lift the heavy monstrosity off and replace it with the lightweight dress. Elastic smocking hugs my waist, and the huge split up the front shows my knees. Lace sleeves with a matching collar and tiered hem give the dress a simple, yet luxurious look. "I love it, but what's going on?"

Shannon releases my French plait leaving my hair loose and wavy. She places a burnt-orange flower headdress on my head and a white crocheted shawl around my shoulders. "You'll need this to keep warm."

"And get rid of *them*." She points to my satin high-heeled shoes. I kick them off and she passes me an ivory pair of flat pumps.

"Am I still getting married?"

"Yes," a voice from behind says.

I turn to see Alex. He hands me a spray of holly and mistletoe tied up with ivory ribbon. "Hello, lovely, where've you been all my life?" he whispers.

"You're so corny." I kiss him on the lips. "But what's going on?"

"That wasn't the wedding *we* wanted. Our parents never even wanted us to get married, so why should they get all their own way? It's our day not theirs."

"I thought something must've happened to you. Mum and Dad said you weren't coming and that you'd …"

"…You know that I'd never let you down. You were the only girl for me from the first time we kissed on Brighton beach. Do you remember that day?"

"As if I could forget."

"And when you took off your maxi coat in Horatio's Bar. Wow, I can still see that black swing mini dress, and those sexy, over knee boots. I knew then..."

I'd felt the same. That night was imprinted on my brain.

We'd wandered along the pebbled beach. Alex held mistletoe over our heads. "You know what this means, don't you?" He kissed me. My very first kiss. I didn't want him to stop.

"Let's go for a paddle," he said.

"In December? Are you mad?"

"Yes." He threw off his socks and shoes and rolled his jeans above his knees. I took my boots off, but I was wearing tights. I looked down at my feet.

119

"Just pull them off. I'll close my eyes and no one else is looking. Ben's far too busy with your friend and the others aren't here."

I slipped off my tights, leaning on Alex. We ran down to the water. "Ouch," I said stumbling over pebbles but when I stepped into the water I screamed. It was so cold. Alex laughed as we both jumped straight out again.

"You're right," he said. "I'm totally mad to have suggested that." He took off his scarf and dried my ice-cold feet. I jerked away from him.

"Sorry, am I tickling you?" He laughed, and started to dry me again.

"Don't." I giggled. "Let me." I took the scarf from him. I slid my bare feet into my boots, shivering.

"Let's get some hot chocolate to warm you up. By the way, where are you from?" he asked.

"Horley. I don't suppose you know it."

"I do. Small world. Me and Ben live down the road in Three Bridges."

I smiled, feeling my cheeks burning up.

Alex grips my hand bringing me back. "Megan, are you listening? I need to go. See you in a minute."

"Yes," I said.

Ben and Lou lead me into the trees. Branches of wood and flowers make a circle. Bikers and their partners stand outside the ring huddled in blankets and Alex is standing inside it.

A woman dressed in a black and red robe strides towards us and says, "Who is it that brings this fair maid to be wed this day?"

"I do," Ben answers.

"Then let it be done."

Portable heaters and flame torches keep the area warm. We follow the woman through a gap in the circle. Ahead is a low tree stump, in use as an altar, where candles and vanilla incense sticks are burning. It's decorated with holly and mistletoe. The woman welcomes Alex and me to the circle. "We gather together on this Winter Solstice..."

I look up into Alex's eyes. "Is this even legal?"

"Of course. She's a celebrant."

I breathe a sigh of relief. This is the wedding *we* both deserve. I smile at the thought of our parents at the church. But all that expense. I do feel a tad guilty.

The celebrant continues with the vows with us answering *I will.* She then takes our hands and ties them with a length of red, orange, and blue cloth. "Red blesses you with fertility, orange with kindness, and blue with loyalty."

Alex and I smile at each other.

"At sacred times and places," the celebrant continues, "our ancestors clasped hands when they wed, and such handfastings witnessed by the gods and the community were lawful, true and binding, as love binds one heart to another."

More vows continue with us answering *I will* or *I am.* The celebrant unties our hands and places the length of cloth across the altar. She takes the rings from Ben and gives one to Alex.

He puts it on my finger. "I promise to love you and be true to you forever."

The celebrant gives me the other ring and I place it on Alex's finger. "I promise to be faithful to you always. You are my soulmate. I will love you forever."

The celebrant continues the service and finally ends with, "May the world be filled with love, beauty and harmony."

"So may it be," everyone answers.

As we stroll back towards the barn, Alex kisses me. "How are you feeling Mrs Chambers?"

"Happy, but...?"

"But what?"

"... all the expense our Mums and Dads went to?"

"I'm not entirely thoughtless." He points towards the barn where waiters and waitresses are heading, laden with boxes. Trailing behind them are our family wedding guests.

"I got Ben to phone your Uncle Geoff and let him know what was happening. But he was given strict instructions not to arrive until after our ceremony. This way our parents get the reception *they* want, but we got the wedding we wanted. Ben and the gang have been out all morning putting up diversion signs to bring all our guests here."

"You thought of everything." I kiss my new husband. "I love you Alex Chambers." Alex's parents are lovely. Doesn't matter to them that they have all that money and a four bedroomed detached while I was brought up in a council house. Why can't Mum and Dad accept Alex? Just because he wears a leather jacket and rides a motorbike doesn't make him a thug. Far from it.

We walk into the barn. Everyone claps. A glorious Christmas tree stands in the corner glistening with lights. A Ceilidh band starts to play.

Mum and Dad stride towards us. *Here goes.*

"You know you nearly gave your father a heart attack?"

Alex's Dad steps forward. "Come on Mr and Mrs McMillan. What's done is done. They could have left us out in the cold completely, couldn't they?" He joins Mum and Dad's hands together and leads them on to the dance floor. "Now, relax. Let your hair down."

The band play a country song. We all hold our arms Gay Gordon style and dance around the room, swinging our partners. Couples part to make an aisle, and the leading pair make an arch. The celebrant's final words ring in my ears, *love beauty and harmony.* My wedding day is complete when Dad pats Alex on the back as we skip through.

Patricia Osborne

Patricia M Osborne, a Chindi author, is in her early 60s, married with grown-up children and grandchildren. She was born in Liverpool, spent time in Bolton as a child, and now lives in West Sussex. In September 2018, Patricia finished an MA in Creative Writing with the University of Brighton and graduated with a Merit.

She is a novelist, poet and also writes short fiction. Many of her poems and short stories have been published in various literary magazines and anthologies. Her debut novel, 'House of Grace, A Family Saga', set in the 1950s/60s was released in March 2017. Her first poetry pamphlet titled 'Taxus Baccata' is to be published shortly by Hedgehog Poetry Press.

Chilblains
by Isabella Muir

18TH DECEMBER 1962

Mum tells everyone who knows me that I was in a rush from the moment I was born. I arrived two weeks before the due date, resulting in panic all round. I've tried to explain to her, and to anyone who will listen, that there's no point in dawdling. Make a decision and act on it.

Which is exactly what I do today on my way home from work. In the ten minutes it takes me to walk from the office to my flat, I decide it's time to ditch my job. A case of getting in first. My boss has dropped enough hints. Apparently, I am 'too pushy' and 'too inquisitive'. (I thought that was the whole point of being a journalist.) Okay, so I've made a few mistakes recently in my haste to hit the press deadline. But everyone knows people often skip over words, the important thing is the gist of the story, the snappy headline. I'm good at those.

There's no way I'm giving Mr 'Perfect' Partridge the pleasure of firing me, just like I've never given any of my ex-boyfriends the chance to dump me. It still makes me smile when I remember the look on Bill's face when I told him we were finished. I'd been the one to ask him out that first time, so it was entirely appropriate that I should be the one to end it. We had nothing in common anyway. It was only his dance moves that had caught my eye and when I walked up to him and said, "Fancy a dance, then?" he nearly fell over with the shock of it. Perhaps he wasn't such a great dancer after all.

The snow starts falling just as I turn the corner into Shoreham Road and by the time I reach the steps down to my basement flat (in truth, it's a bedsit) the steps have disappeared, to be replaced with something that more closely resembles a ski slope. I slide down in a fairly ungainly manner, but manage to avoid tipping over, which could well have ruined my latest acquisition. Mary Quant's fashion genius had recently arrived here in Brighton and I had been at the front of the queue, handing over the best part of a week's wages for my beautiful mac.

Once inside my little haven of chaos, I fill the kettle, stick it on the gas and then there are more decisions to make. No job, no money. No money, no rent. Since I moved into Flat 1b, just under a year ago, I've made the place pretty cosy, mainly courtesy of other people's throwaways. I've also proved to Mum that I can do the whole independence thing. Now it looks as though I'll have to leave the bright lights of Brighton and return to the slightly duller ones of Hastings. The worst bit will be having to listen to Mum saying, 'I told you so'.

I turn the volume dial on my transistor radio up to maximum and listen to The Beatles sing out *Love me do*. Unfortunately, it will now be even longer before I can afford my own record player. Still, once I'm back in Hastings, at least I'll have the chance to use Mum's.

19TH DECEMBER

I have to practically dig my way out of the bedsit this morning. The snow fell throughout the night and drifted down into my little basement yard, climbing at least one third of the way up my front door.

I shift the worst of it and make a slower than usual plod into the newspaper offices, but I still manage to arrive before Mr Partridge. I put my resignation letter in a prominent position on his desk, give Marcus and Sally hugs and wish them well. It'll be up to them now to cover all those boring WI meetings and village fetes. Someone has to do it and it will no longer be me. I give them Mum's address and they promise to keep in touch, but I know they won't, or at best it's highly unlikely.

A trudge back through the snow to the bedsit to throw my few belongings into the old battered suitcase that Mum donated to me when I left. Anything that doesn't fit in the case I'll leave for the next fun seeker.

There's time to drop round to the landlord with the week's rent and a note to say I'm off in a day or two. Then, with more snow falling, I push my way into Fred's Café. The welcome warmth and smell of frying envelops me, like a big hug. I make my first mug of coffee last as long as possible; it's at least an hour before Stu will be home from work. But when the waitress hovers near my table for the third time, I decide it's safer to order another coffee, accompanied by a couple of rounds of buttered toast.

Fred's Café was where Stu brought me for our first date.

"Really pushing the boat out then?" I'd teased him about it every time we walked past. His flat is just opposite.

Actually, this is only the second time I've been inside in the ten weeks we've been going out together - my longest ever relationship.

It's not such a big deal. I'll just tell him I'm going back to Hastings. We'll have a kiss and he'll be another one to promise to keep in touch, but he won't.

It was a newspaper that brought us together – literally. We both went to grab a copy of *The Guardian* at the same moment. Instead of apologising, he launched into a speech about how politicians don't care about us 'little people'. When he finally stopped speaking, I told him I agreed with every word he'd uttered. It wasn't flattery, although I definitely fancied him. But what he said made sense. We soon joined the rest of the world, as we collectively held our breath for fourteen days while President Kennedy and Kruschev decided if they were going to obliterate the world in a nuclear war. By the time the worst of that was over we had kind of clicked.

We'd sat on a freezing Brighton beach, trying to imagine being blown to pieces. He talked about his hopes and dreams and I listened. I told him my plans for five, ten and fifteen years from now and he just laughed. "Sometimes you need to let things flow; don't be in such a rush."

Where have I heard that before?

He asked me if I missed home. Not really. Growing up, right next door to Hastings Station, watching the trains out of my bedroom window, must have given me itchy feet.

"Trains rattling past don't keep you awake?"

"It's like the best lullaby," I tell him and mean it.

So, yes, it's a shame, but the decision is made and there's no point revisiting it. Anyway, Stu made it clear from the beginning that he didn't think long-term.

"Where's home for you, then?" I'd asked him that day on the beach.

"Here for now. When I'm bored, I'll move on."

So, here I am, getting in first.

20TH DECEMBER

It pretty much went as I'd expected. Except for the snow. I had never imagined that frozen water could create so much trouble. It's very pretty, but it just stops everything from moving.

Buses are cancelled and I've never been brave enough to learn to drive. Even if I had managed it, I couldn't afford a car on a junior reporter's wages. Luckily, the trains are still running. Stu offers to walk with me to the station. I'm not great on goodbyes and he says he isn't either, which makes for a rather awkward hug. I slip a piece of paper into his jacket pocket (no harm in him having Mum's phone number, just in case) and then nearly fall over as I dash onto the icy platform. I don't turn around to wave; keep moving forward, that's my motto.

The train journey gives me time to mull over yesterday's conversation with Stu. I kept it all pretty light-hearted, told him that the past ten weeks had been fun, but that it was time for us both to see what else life had in store. I told a bit of a white lie when I said Mum had been pestering me to go back to Hastings. He laughed and said she needs to be careful what she wishes for. That little dig was probably referring to the state of my bedsit. I invited him back once, after we'd been to the cinema to see the latest Bond film. It was a spur of the moment thing, but then Stu made me jump out of my skin when he shouted out, just as I opened the door to the bedsit.

"Oh God, you've been burgled."

I looked around and wondered what made him think that. Everything was just as I had left it that morning. I had to apologise for the place being such a pigsty and he just started to laugh and wouldn't stop until I threatened to tip a bowl of water over his head. Which, I suppose, would have set the seal on the mess, and on the evening. When he finally did stop laughing the rest of the evening (and night) was pretty much perfect.

But everyone knows perfect doesn't last.

21ST DECEMBER

It's been a week of firsts. First time I've walked out on a job, a flat and a fella in the space of a few days. First time I've wondered whether I've made a mistake, but not about the job or the flat.

Now I'm back with Mum I'm going to carry on breaking new ground. Once she leaves for work I intend to prepare a surprise tea for her. This will require a list (list-making is not my forte, in fact, I can't remember the last time I made one).

I had planned to make the special tea yesterday when I arrived. The idea was to have the table laid, covered with her favourite things, kettle on the hob, fire crackling in the grate for when she got home from work. But the journey had exhausted me. The snowfall hadn't stopped the trains running, but they had certainly slowed them down. All I wanted to do was soak in a hot bath. Trouble was I was still soaking when I heard Mum put her key in the front door. I listened to her tentative steps along the hallway to the kitchen. She would have seen my boots. I'd kicked them off and left them lying just inside the front door. An immediate giveaway.

"Patsy?" There was a mixture of hopefulness and anxiety in her voice. I could imagine her thinking, 'Surely a burglar wouldn't choose knee-high white PVC boots and thoughtfully remove them on entry.'

"I'm in the bath." As I called out to her I had already dragged myself away from the warm suds, wrapped a towel around me and padded, still slightly damp-footed, to the top of the stairs.

Then it was hugs and 'Why didn't you let me know you were coming?' and an evening of catching up, with Mum offering to make my favourite supper and asking me what I fancied for Christmas dinner.

But today is going to be different. At least that's my plan until I open the door and feel the Siberian blast. I close the door. Maybe there's enough food in the larder for me to knock up something without having to venture out. And it won't hurt to be by the phone, because you just never know.

22ND DECEMBER

Last night the weather really took hold. Blizzards and gale-force winds combined, resulting in power lines coming down across the south coast. The only news we can get now is via the transistor radio, where forecasters threaten more of the same, on and on, until we'll be living in a frozen wasteland. Apparently there are eight-foot high snow drifts in places. Great. Nothing and no one moving anywhere.

23RD DECEMBER

It's actually kind of cosy. We have candles to brighten up the dark spaces and plenty of coal for the fire.

I spent a long time this morning standing in the garden, letting the snowflakes land on me, resisting the temptation to move, to fidget. I was becoming a real, live, snow woman.

By the time I came inside I had lost most of the feeling in my fingers and toes. And then I remembered what Mum had told me every winter – about how to avoid chilblains. You have to take things slowly, let the blood flow from your heart, until it reaches all the extremities in its own gradual way, making them come alive again. If you rush at trying to fix it all, then you will end up hurting.

That wasn't all she taught me. I must have been about nine or ten when I last helped to make mince pies. I'd forgotten how much fun it is. So now here we are, with her slowly rolling out the pastry and me slowly spooning in the mincemeat. She uses a taper to light the gas, lets the heat build and then the best part is when the oven door opens to reveal the golden baked delights. She smacks my fingers when I try to grab one.

She'd put her order in for the turkey ages ago, so all we had to do yesterday was wander round to the butcher's and the greengrocers, returning laden with enough food to keep us going until new year at least.

"Did you guess I'd be home for Christmas then?" I challenge her. "That's an awfully large turkey for one person."

All I get in response is a knowing smile.

The larder is filled with all my favourites: lime marmalade, custard creams, and Cadbury's chocolate fingers. There is even a jar of mustard piccalilli.

Sunday evening, we turn the transistor radio up loud and sing along to Cliff and Elvis. She jumps up and grabs my hand.

"Come on, let's do *The Mashed Potato*." She swings me around, swivelling and stepping back and forth.

"When did you learn this?" We laugh as we bump into each other.

The music is so loud that even if the phone could ring, even if the phone lines hadn't been felled by the worst winter I can remember, we wouldn't hear it.

CHRISTMAS EVE

He merely shrugs and laughs when we ask him how he got here. How he overcame the blizzards, slow trains, no trains, no power. Precisely ten hours after he knocked on the door, we are sitting in the kitchen, candles dripping wax onto the wooden table, the oven door open for us to enjoy the heat from the gas flames.

Mum has gone up to bed, says she doesn't want to be awake at midnight in case Santa catches her with her eyes open.

"Blow the candles out before you come up to bed, or you'll burn the house down," she says, as much to Stu as to me.

"Just a visit?" I ask him.

He shakes his head. "I think you know the answer to that. Anyway, falling asleep to the rattle of trains, sounds perfect to me."

"I thought with the phone lines down…"

"That piece of paper."

I attempt a quizzical look, but I'm guessing it looks more like I'm trying to suppress a sneeze.

"There was nothing on it." He takes the scrap of notepaper from his jacket pocket and shows me both sides – blank.

Rushing about means sometimes you make mistakes. And there's always the danger of chilblains.

Isabella Muir

Isabella Muir, a Chindi author, has been surrounded by books her whole life. For twenty-five years she worked as a technical editor and then, having successfully completed her MA in Professional Writing, she was inspired to focus on fiction writing.

Her passion for the sights, sounds and experiences of the 1960s, provides the perfect inspiration for her *Sussex Crime Mystery* series of novels, which feature young librarian and amateur sleuth, Janie Juke, who has a passion for Agatha Christie's Hercule Poirot. Isabella is half-Italian and so was delighted to have the *Sussex Crime Mystery* series translated into Italian and made available for sale in Rome bookshops.

Isabella's latest standalone novel, *The Forgotten Children,* explores family life in the 1960s, highlighting the British policy of sending unaccompanied children to Australia, which inflicted emotional damage that continues to the present day.

Find out more by visiting: https://isabellamuir.com/

The Gift
by Susanne Haywood

It had been a trying night, he reflected, as he changed course towards the southwest and his last stop. From the very start, his annual journey had been beset with problems. First the broken harness, which should have been picked up weeks ago, during the routine inspection. *Slapdash* was the word that sprang to mind; you had to be meticulous with a complex harness for eight animals. He gave a little sniff of annoyance. Helpers really weren't what they used to be. Nothing was. Then his list had disappeared, along with his glasses, and not the slightest idea where he'd last seen them. By the time his wife had finally located them in his coat pocket and the last few parcels had been loaded, he was running dangerously late.

Maybe he was getting too old for this job. But who else would take over such a thankless task? What kind of fulfilment lay in the production of beautiful things all year if you then had to spend an entire night out of bed – at his age – delivering them to people who, as far as he could see, often took them for granted or even put them away, never to be seen again? When had anyone ever given *him* anything? Gallons of cheap sherry, yes, and tons of shop-bought mince-pies of inferior quality that gave him indigestion until Easter. A proper gift, just for him, from their hearts was what he longed for, to motivate him for another year of toil. But fat chance, he sniffed as he drew his red coat tighter around his ample waist and gave the reins a flick. They hadn't done so in centuries. Why would they start now?

Fortunately, it was a still night, not a breath of wind, so they had been able to make up time, particularly once the bulk of the load was shed, and his mood had gradually improved. His last stop was one he actually looked forward to, which was why he left it to the very end each year. As the big sleigh smoothly rode the sky above the South Downs, the reindeer now tired and no longer up to their tricks of friskier moments earlier in the night, he looked about him and couldn't help sighing with pleasure at the scenery below.

It was a night of crackling cold. The frost had dabbed trees and open fields with a silvery white, and the full moon outlined the soft silhouette of the hills against the night sky. Flocks of sheep were huddling together under the protective branches of the mighty trees that dotted the hillside; and an owl hooted a welcome.

His heart lifted a little more when the big old house came into view, dark and snug in its hollow, wrapped securely in several layers of shrubbery immaculately trimmed to mirror the gentle curves of the Downs. The glass of the greenhouses sparkled in the moonlight; smartly edged paths meandered among the flowerbeds; the little brook was a silver ribbon guiding him along. He loved everything about the place, from its perfect situation in the valley to the cosy drawing room, where he hoped to spend a peaceful half hour at the end of his long night's work, doing justice to the mulled wine kept hot for him in a thermos flask – no sherry here, thank goodness! – and the delicious home-made mince pies always set out for him on a small table by one of the sofas. Now that was a touch of class. There might also be fat bunches of organically grown carrots from the kitchen gardens for his reindeer.

The roof was tricky to negotiate due to the battlements, but he had plenty of practice and managed to tuck sleigh and reindeer neatly in between the row of chimneys.

"Wait!" he commanded, and with a piercing clatter of bells that threatened to wake up the entire village, the eight reindeer settled down, looking mulish, but too tired to rebel. He shouldered his last sack – not a very big one; there hadn't been any children in the house for many years – and began his descent down the chimney. The last embers of an earlier fire were glowing gently beneath him, warming his legs as he went down. Hardly any smoke; not like other chimneys where he'd had to brave billowing black clouds and vicious flames – risky, in spite of his fire-retardant suit.

The sight that met him as he jumped on to the hearth rug was just what he'd expected: the large, elegant room with its tall windows curtained against the cold; the paintings, weapons and coats of arms gleaming on the panelled walls; the grand piano in its alcove with a book of Christmas songs open on the stand; the soft carpets; and the tall tree tastefully decorated with golden baubles. With a grunt of relief, he lowered himself into his favourite sofa, poured a large goblet of mulled wine and bit into his first mince pie. There were three, and he would not be leaving any. At long last, the spirit of Christmas that had eluded him all night began to creep cautiously into his heart. Maybe it had all been worth it again, after all?

He was just taking a bite out of his second mince pie when a loud meow startled him and, looking up, he saw a large, fluffy cat sitting on the hearth rug, in the very spot where he'd just landed moments ago. A tortoiseshell with a long, silky coat and green eyes that fixed him with a probing stare.

"Hullo there, cat," he said, with a very full mouth. "I haven't met you before. Have you moved in during the year? I bet you're wondering what I'm doing here?"

The cat blinked in agreement.

"I'm a figure of myth and legend who brings presents once a year, on Christmas Eve." He rattled it off in the bored tone of one who is repeating a well-practised phrase for the umpteenth time and gestured at the plump red sack leaning against the side of the sofa. "And much thanks I get for it," he added morosely.

The cat approached him doubtfully, sniffed at the sack, then sat back as though her mind was made up, arranged her tail delicately around her paws and gave him a long look that reached down into his very soul. It was intensely irritating and he tried to resist, but found he couldn't. A deep warmth began to spread in his chest and rose all the way to his cheeks. *She knows how I feel; she understands.* But no; it couldn't be. He quickly shook his head to get rid of the silly thought.

"You think there's something in there for you?" he grunted, drawing his bushy eyebrows together in the way that never failed to spread fear among his helpers. "Now why would I bring something for you, tell me that?"

The bright green eyes closed for a moment, giving the cat a pained expression. Then she turned abruptly and disappeared through the open door. Without her, the room seemed different, as though a light had been snuffed out and all the warmth that had been building inside him had been extinguished along with it.

"That's that then. Typical!" he shrugged and picked up the third mince pie.

But he had hardly bitten into it when the cat was back, carrying a toy mouse in her mouth, which she carefully placed at his feet. He almost choked on his mince pie in surprise.

"Good Lord!" he spluttered, "is that for me?"

The cat gave a barely perceptible nod. He looked more closely at the mouse. It was beautifully made of soft, grey felt and had a long, shiny rubber tail, very realistic, and silky whiskers. Surely every cat's dream? But she was giving it to him. The thing he had been waiting for, had hardly dared hope for after centuries of disappointment, had happened: someone had given him a gift, from the heart. He cleared his throat in order to hide the unexpected emotion that threatened to uproot his well-established gruffness.

"I suppose I'd better see whether I've got something in my sack for you, then," he muttered, suddenly embarrassed by his rudeness earlier.

He sank his arm deep inside the sack and rummaged about. The cat waited politely. At length, he pulled out a parcel with a green bow on top that exactly matched the colour of the cat's eyes and a label that read *Buffy* in big gold letters, and put it down in front of her.

"Yours I believe, my friend. I hope you like it."

The cat unceremoniously tore off bow and paper with her sharp claws to reveal a shallow china dish decorated

140

with colourful fish and filled to the brim with cream. She took one lick, gave an appreciative chirrup and continued lapping contentedly, making little smacking noises.

An odd tremor went through his facial muscles. The corners of his mouth twitched upwards, the wrinkles around his eyes contracted, and before he could stop himself, he was smiling. This had not happened for at least a hundred years, but it felt amazing.

"Seems like I chose the right gift for you," he chortled as he let the remaining contents of the sack tumble out all over the hearth rug. "Let's hope I've done equally well for the humans."

With great tenderness, he lifted his toy mouse by its tail and lowered it into the empty sack, pushed the remainder of the mince pie into his mouth and, as the cat lovingly licked the bottom of her new bowl, began the steep climb back up the chimney. But he felt feathery-light and nimble, and the climb, normally so challenging, hardly tired him at all. As he popped out at the top and stepped on to the roof, the air seemed milder and the reindeer looked pleased to see him. They stood up dutifully, anticipating his command, with a pretty jingle of bells. He swung himself on to the sleigh, flicked the reins and, as the sleigh lifted off the roof, swept across the park and took a northerly direction, he pulled off his hat, whirled it in the air with uncharacteristic recklessness and yelled "Merry Christmas, West Dean! Merry Christmas, everyone!"

Susanne Haywood

Susanne Haywood, a Chindi author, was born and bred in Austria. She is married with three grown-up children and lives in West Sussex.

Susanne has worked at universities in Austria, the UK and Australia, both as an academic and in senior management. She is now retired and devoting more time to her passion for writing, which she does in English and German.

Following a number of academic publications on the subject of National Socialist ideology in German 1920s children's literature, Susanne independently published her semi-autobiographical novel in 2015. *Tigger: Memoirs of a Cosmopolitan Cat* tracks the Haywoods' international moves from the perspective of the family cat. The book has been well received and is in its second print run. Since then, Susanne has completed a book club/crime novel set in Australia, which she is currently seeking to place with a publisher and is now writing an historical novel set during World War II.

When the Bee Choir Sings
by Rosemary Noble

"What's happening?" she murmured, as a peal of bells roused her into wakefulness.

Lottie's first thought was invasion, but Boney's armies had been defeated years before. Her creaking bones were no longer those of a young girl cheering the ships home, with red coats lining the decks and the pubs of old Portsmouth ringing with the drunken cheers of a hero's welcome.

Her memories cleared. Could it be Christmas? Wincing with pain, she climbed from the scratchy blankets and hobbled to the window, set too high to see anything but a flickering star. The bells continued to ring, shattering the regime of silence so strictly maintained. Despite her shivering, Lottie listened intently, revelling in the joyful sound. She pictured her parish church, its squat steeple nestling underneath the Downs, the buttresses like the ribs of a soaring buzzard. Closing her eyes, she began to hum, 'I saw three ships come sailing in' and was transported inside the nave. Sitting once again on a hard, wooden pew, a babe in her arms, tiny boys at either side, she pointed at the tendrils of leaves and flowers decorating the ceiling, the trumpets of the daffodils their favourite. Lottie's breath caught in her throat; she could almost feel Fred's arm around her. Him long since in his grave.

The sound of a child snivelling nearby gave her goose bumps. Opening her eyes, she peered around in the darkness, thinking little Charlie or Eddie needed her. The mournful cry was muted by the solid brick walls. It was the girl next door. Lottie leant to place her hands against the wall and crooned with her mouth against the cold, whitewashed plaster. Had she been able, she would have taken the girl on her knee to comfort her. The poor thing missed her mother. A sour smell of loneliness permeated the bricks.

Silence returned, no comfort in that. Lottie longed for noise, any noise. A church full of singing; market sellers calling out their wares; the screech of children's laughter, the louder the better. Noise had leached out of this place until the beating of a broken heart, a shuffling shoe against the cold flagstones and the clink of a spoon on an enamel plate roared in her ears.

Lottie crept back to bed. Midnight, long hours stretched ahead unless she could lull herself back to sleep. Think of good times, of Christmases past; her first as a newlywed in her tiny cottage in Boxgrove, with her eldest sucking on her breast and Fred, her bonny boy, blue eyes sparkling with pride, teasing her into laughter.

"Can you hear them, my love?" he had said to her.

"What?" she had asked.

"The bee choir in its hive. Everyone knows it sings at Christmas."

All Lottie could hear was the log fire crackling in its hearth and the wind tearing at the solitary oiled-paper windowpane. "In Sussex, maybe, Fred," she had laughed. "Not in Portsmouth. Honeybees are strangers to the flowerless lanes of Portsmouth."

"No, no, listen."

144

She tried again; the snuffles of her nuzzling baby she could hear. Wait! Was that the faint strain of a melody from somewhere outside?

Her husband caught her hand and nodded. "You hear them now." He winked.

"Don't be daft, that must be a choir practising for the service tomorrow."

"Maybe or maybe not." It was a trick he played each year of their marriage. She never tired of it.

They used to deck the cottage with holly and mistletoe from the old Stane Street track. On a frosty morning, the lane through the woods looked magical, each twig festooned with a cobweb of white, laced rime. As their boots crunched through the frozen cartwheel puddles, Fred would scare her and the boys with tales of the ghosts of soldiers guarding the road up to London, the same ones who'd built the walls around Chichester more than a thousand years ago, before even the priory was built. Lottie remembered her boys' wide stare and their squeals of terror at the thought of spectres amongst the tall beech trees overlooking the dirt road. She had always suspected the stories of ghosts were sewn by smugglers, keen to avoid prying eyes on those nights when they moved the brandy from the coast towards London. Many's the night her husband had left her bed for a few hours around midnight. She asked no questions, only grateful for the few shillings which kept them from hunger. Happy days.

Lottie sighed and moved awkwardly on the straw mattress. Her wedding was around the time the old king died. "I'm as old as the century," she murmured, "and I remember the celebrations when the regent, fat George, we called him, came to the throne. Not that I ever saw him; Boxgrove is the other side of Sussex from his fanciful palace, but I heard about it. Who didn't?" A pedlar had tried to describe it to her once, all circular domes, columns and something called minarets. She couldn't imagine it but itched to see it. She fell asleep knowing that would never happen.

A new day. Christmas morn. The bells were ringing in triumph. Would there be any change in the routine? Empty her night bucket, sweep the floor, a meagre breakfast of tea, bread, oatmeal if they were lucky, a chapel service no doubt. The call to prayers came sooner than she thought. With her stomach grumbling its displeasure, she filed into the bleak chapel. No festive cheer lightened its stone walls and blackened pews where the inmates sat apart, huddled in their isolation. No 'Happy Christmas, God be with you on this blessed morn'. Only her memories to keep her company.

Christmas should be a time of hope, hope that things will be better next year. How her boys had loved to go a-wassailing to the apple orchards, to beat on the gnarled trees and sing for a howling good crop. The family used to walk into Chichester with their neighbours to watch the mummers perform their play around the old Market Cross, before setting off for the grand houses where the players would be plied with food and drink. If Fred had a few pennies to spare, he'd buy hot chestnuts to warm their hands and their stomachs before heading home. The family didn't do so badly in those early days. Bread was just about affordable; Lottie grew a few vegetables and herbs in the patch outside their cottage, an occasional rabbit from the poacher and sometimes a hunk of cheese, or a slab of fat bacon when a neighbour slaughtered the pig that they had all donated their slops to rear.

The good times, the best of times.

It was the threshing machines and three bad harvests one after the other which did for them. The winter work dried to less than a trickle. The farmers blamed the tithes for the fall in wages as the men protested.

"What are we to do? How are we supposed to live? How are my babies to survive?" She had begged her husband for answers. His shoulders slumped, fists balled by his sides, a greyness in his face that spoke of despair. All around their neighbours grew more scared, more hungry, more desperate.

Then the trouble began. It began like a whisper on the breeze, no more than the first russet autumn leaf swept up to float under the wooden planks of their door and finding a home on their cold hearth, an augur of winter to come.

Then it became a buzzing, like bees around a lavender bush, something to be watched and welcomed, a promise of sweetness. Could they, dare they make a difference? Fred brought the gossip back from an ale house in Tangmere. There'd been trouble in Kent, letters had been written by a mysterious Captain Swing, labourers had taken matters into their own hands and landowners were scared, some raising wages rather than risking being burnt out.

Finally, it became a roar as the villagers caught sight of flames and plumes of smoke from burning hayricks far away, south of the Downs towards Worthing. Men with sledgehammers were on the march around Fishbourne and Bosham to the west. Neighbours listened open-mouthed until someone said they too must rise up and demand change from the lord. Words were spoken, rousing words, words to get the blood boiling in their veins and their hearts beating with anger. This was the time to stop the pain of hunger in their children's bellies. How long could they live on nettle soup?

They had marched towards Halnaker Hill. High up they stood, by the windmill, the newly harvested fields beneath their feet. Fields they would have scoured for grain in bygone years. Grain enough to give a few loaves of bread; now all that was left was fit only for starlings to scratch at. Dames in the village used to tell of a time when the church bells rang to signal gleaning was to begin, the farmer willing to share his bounty with his workers. Those days had disappeared. They were told that the mill towns of the north needed all of the wheat to feed their workers. The labourers of Sussex were left to cry on that hillside.

"What about us? Don't we need bread too?"

Lottie looked up towards the chaplain in his pulpit. Could he see the pain in her breast? She cast her eyes down again, the tears in her eyes dropped unnoticed. The disgust in his voice as he spoke of their sins scarcely matched the rage of the men as they spoke of their injustices that day: of the government barring the imports of cheap corn to feed them, of the lowering of wages, of the lack of parish assistance.

Tempers rose throughout that afternoon sixteen years before. Lottie had simmered with rage that someone would choose to keep her children hungry for the sake of their own pocket. She knew naught of what went on in London, but it didn't seem right that some have everything and others nothing. The vicar had stomped uphill. Red-faced and sweating despite the November chill, he tried to calm things by reminding them that their lot on earth was ordained by God and to expect their reward in heaven. The men were having none of it. He was booed and heckled until he left, no doubt to raise the alarm. What now, they had wondered? Should they fire the hayricks?

Doubt and fear had swept through Lottie. She leant into her husband, reminding him of the baby she was carrying. If cudgels were to be taken up against the landowners and fires set, selfishly she wanted others to do it, not him.

"Come away, Fred. Let the men with no babies at home take up arms."

"No, Lottie. We all must fight or none at all. Go home to our little ones. Guard them well."

Yet she had stayed, too afraid for her man.

A hunting horn had sounded and, in a swirl of dust, up galloped a commanding figure, all booted and suited in finery.

"T'is the Lord of the Manor," someone shouted. Lottie gawped like a fish to see him.

"Go now," said her husband. "Get away back home. This is no place for you."

She and the other women stumbled down the hill, through the pack of horses bearing farmers with stout sticks and horse whips. Lottie was knocked to the ground by one of them. Winded, she watched as they set upon their unarmed menfolk. What could they do against the Lord and his men, tired and ill-fed as they were? Lottie crawled into a ditch by the hedge, feeling the blood trickling down her legs, praying that her husband would not be killed as they had surely killed her babe.

The fight soon over, the Lord sat back on his horse and harangued the men. They had no business gathering on his land. He had every right to defend his property against a mob of lawless ingrates. Had they a grievance, they ought to address his land agent. His anger subsided as the men lay battered and bruised on the ground. The Lord promised he would listen later, when he had time and his dinner wasn't waiting. He and his men rode away down the hill cheering and whooping, leaving carnage behind them. A hero of the French wars, someone once called him. Were his workers Boney's men to be treated so?

She must have fallen into a stupor because she didn't remember the men leaving the hill. After first limping all the way home, her husband had found her groaning like a sick cow as pains gripped her belly. He held her against him and howled for help, but none came. She was too far gone to move.

He was born perfect, too puny to take his first breath, too innocent to live. Lottie had felt his heart flutter and then still, though she tried to massage him back to life. They wrapped him in her husband's kerchief to take home

150

to bury. That field, bathed in her family's blood, would grow fine crops for the Lord the following harvest.

Lottie had made a vow that day. One she had kept. No child of hers would be a farm labourer. She would give all that she had to make that happen.

The sermon ended. The prisoners shuffled on their seats before standing to sing or pretend to. Lottie was familiar with the tune, *Christians Awake*, but her heart would not allow her to say the words. It remained in the ditch on that hillside. Had it ever left? No one had been given a chance to salute her last baby.

Proudly, she raised her head to the chaplain as she filed out back to her cell. My sins are the sins of survival, of sacrifice so that my children may thrive. I may not live to see them again, but I have seen them safely settled, she thought.

The cleric met her eyes briefly, expecting what? Repentance, abjection. His cold, grey eyes flickered to see her ruddy face, scored with the deep lines of poverty, unbowed, unbroken, a gap-toothed grin, her own small victory.

Back in her cell, Lottie sat on the three-legged stool with a blanket wrapped tight around her. She began to hum, a made-up song, a song befitting a new life, a new country. One thing she knew, next Christmas she would feel the warmth of the sun on her face. She closed her eyes to picture the tales she had been told in her youth by returning sailors of a strange land at the far ends of the earth. A land where the seasons are topsy-turvy, where birds laugh, animals hop, daisies grow into great bushes, where the sea shimmers with light, and brightly coloured parrots flit amongst tall, brooding trees.

There, at Christmas, surely an entire choir of bees would sing an ancient song as they feasted on the nectar of a thousand flowers dancing in the warm breeze of Van Diemen's Land. Lottie smiled as she imagined her grave set amongst such wonders. There she would rest content.

Author's note – I met a descendant of Lottie's in Tasmania in 2018 and was inspired to write this story. Lottie, a washerwoman, died a year after arriving in 1848.

Rosemary Noble

Rosemary Noble, originally from Lincolnshire, moved to Sussex thirty-five years ago. She is the author of four historical sagas, including the popular Currency Girls Series set in England and Australia. She is a Director of Chindi Authors' Network and a volunteer researcher for the Australian Founders and Survivors Project run by the University of Melbourne in conjunction with the Female Convicts Research Group.

Prior to retirement, she was a university and college librarian, but now claims to be busier than ever. She is currently writing a children's book at the request of her granddaughter and a new novel set in Sussex – a mixture of modern and historical themes. She also runs Ghost Tours of Littlehampton.

Read her blog at https://rosemarynoble.wordpress.com/

The Mystery of the Phantom Santa
by Peter Bartram

"You don't need to ask me what I want for Christmas," said Frank Figgis.

He was holding the stub of Woodbine ostentatiously between his thumb and forefinger. He eased the dog-end between his lips and took a long drag. The ash dropped off and fluttered down his waistcoat like an early snow flurry.

"An ashtray?" I suggested.

Figgis harrumphed. He stubbed the dog-end out on the edge of his desk and tossed it into his waste bin.

Figgis was news editor of the *Evening Chronicle*. We were sitting in his office. It was the day before Christmas Eve.

"Never mind that," he said, brushing the ash off his waistcoat. "What I want to know is what you've got planned for the Christmas Eve edition."

It was a question I dreaded every year. Traditionally, tomorrow's paper would be full of Christmas-themed stories.

It wasn't hard to find a seasonal yarn if you were the paper's business reporter. She'd be telling us that tills were ringing in the town's shops which had had their best Christmas trading ever. Just as she had last year.

And simple if you were running the woman's page. No doubt we'd be learning about another ten exciting things we could do with left-over turkey.

But not such a breeze if, like me, your byline read Colin Crampton, crime correspondent. My Christmas staple was the reheated favourite about thieves who broke into a house and stole the kiddies' presents from under the tree. It helped if they were orphans (the kiddies that is, not the thieves).

But this year, it seemed as though they'd knocked off early for the holiday (the thieves, not the kiddies). The orphans would be getting their stockings stuffed full by Santa. I had no story.

So I looked Figgis in the eye and said: "I'm working on something. I think it could be big."

"Yes, and this," he reached for another Woodbine, "is a *Romeo y Julieta* cigar."

I stomped back to the newsroom feeling like the cracker that didn't go bang.

I was angry with myself for not lining up a seasonal story for the Christmas Eve edition. I had to find something but time was running out.

Sally Martin, who wrote for the woman's page, bumped into me as I barged through the newsroom's swing doors.

"You look as though you've just swallowed the sixpence from the Christmas pud," she said.

"Worse," I said.

She arched an eyebrow. "Figgis' Christmas story?"

I nodded.

"You haven't got one?" she said.

I nodded again.

"So you'll be paying the Figgis' Yuletide fine?"

"Looks like I've no choice," I said.

It had been a tradition on the paper since before I joined that you either handed in a Christmas story on the twenty-fourth of December or paid Figgis a fine of one hundred Woodbines. Nobody knew when the tradition had started. But, then, nobody had been on the paper as long as Figgis. He'd probably started it himself. Anything to get more free smokes. But I was determined he wasn't getting any from me.

Sally shrugged. "It's happened to all of us. By the way, can you think of a tenth way to use left-over turkey? I've got nine already."

"Only one," I said. "And it involves Frank Figgis. But I'm not sure there's a kitchen utensil for what I've got in mind."

I crossed to my desk and slumped into my old captain's chair. I brushed a stray strand of tinsel that had fallen from the decorations off my typewriter.

There were a couple of messages to call contacts. I recognised the names. They were time-wasters and would be angling for a Christmas drink on the strength of a feeble tip-off that wouldn't even make a paragraph. I decided to ignore them.

Instead, I picked up the phone and dialled a number at Brighton police station.

The phone was answered after three rings. "Detective Inspector Ted Wilson."

"What do you get if you cross Father Christmas with a detective?" I said.

"Santa Clues," he said. "We had those crackers at the CID's Christmas bash last night. Presumably you've not just called to tell weak jokes?"

"When you weren't carousing, did you happen to come across any festive crime?" I said. "I'm looking for a story with a seasonal theme."

A throaty chuckle came down the line. "Well, I've got good news for you. It looks as though 1963 is going to be the quietest Christmas I've known since I joined this station. Looks like the criminal classes have taken on board that bit about peace and goodwill to all men."

"Too bad," I said. "Let me know if you hear of anything."

"What did Cinderella say when the developers mislaid her photos?" he said.

"Some day my prints will come," I said.

I replaced the receiver.

Twenty minutes later I was sitting on a bench in the Royal Pavilion gardens.

I needed time to think away from the hurly-burly of the office.

It was a crisp morning with December sun low in the sky. Frost glistened on the dome and minarets of the Royal Pavilion.

I could hear the Sally Army band in New Road playing carols. They were on *In the Bleak Midwinter*. Their choice matched my mood.

A young lad was kicking a football about on the grass. He dribbled past the flower bed and scored a goal between an oak tree and a sign reading 'No ball games'.

I rummaged in my pocket, pulled out my notebook and flipped back through the pages. I was looking for something – anything – that I'd overlooked which I might turn into a Christmas story. There'd been no shortage of crime in Brighton in the past few weeks.

There was the capture of Big Brucie Dangerfield who'd shot a young police constable during a bank raid. He'd been tried for murder - and was now in Wormwood Scrubs awaiting the hangman's noose.

And I hadn't forgotten the Newhaven bonded warehouse heist, where thieves had made off with a haul of ten thousand Gauloises cigarettes. They'd brained the night-watchman who'd died two days later from his injuries. So now police were mounting a murder hunt.

Both great crime stories, but nothing with a Christmas theme...

Ooouf! A football cannoned into me and I dropped my notebook.

The young lad ran up. He was dressed in a thick brown jumper and short trousers. He looked about eight years old. His lips were pursed and his eyes were worried. He picked up the notebook and handed it to me.

"Sorry, mister," he said.

I grinned. "Did I save a goal?"

"Didn't mean to kick it this way. Can I have my ball back?" he said.

I tossed the ball in the air and caught it.

"I'll tell you a secret if you give it to me," he said.

I handed him the football. "I like secrets," I said.

"I've seen Father Christmas," he said.

"Coming down the chimney, was he?"

"No. He was out the back of our house. By the garages. But he had a sack and a beard."

"And a red coat?"

158

"I couldn't see the colour. But it came right down to the ground. It was dark. I was looking out of my bedroom window. My Mum says I should've been in bed."

"Where is your Mum?" I looked around.

A woman wearing an old grey coat and with a scarf tied over her head was hurrying across the grass.

"Billy, come here," she called out. "I told you not to run off."

She came up, panting slightly. She had a pinched face with thin lips. "Sorry if he's been annoying you," she said. The scowl on her face said she didn't much care whether he'd been annoying me or not.

"Not at all," I said. "He's been telling me that he's seen Father Christmas."

She grabbed Billy's hand and shook his arm roughly. "I've told you not to tell tales," she said.

She turned to me: "Ignore him. He invents things."

"But I did see Father Christmas. Three nights in a row," Billy protested.

"For the last time, you did not see Father Christmas." There was a harsh rasp in her voice.

"This is the time of year to indulge children's fantasies," I said.

She faced me and the look on her thin face was pitched somewhere between defiant and evasive. "Not those kinds of fantasies," she said. "Now, if you'll excuse me."

She tugged Billy's arm. "Come on, we've got to go and buy the turkey and Brussels sprouts."

Billy grinned a kind of lop-sided grin at me and followed his Mum.

159

"Do turkeys come from Turkey?" I heard him say as they moved off towards North Street.

"No."

"Where do turkeys come from if they don't come from Turkey?"

"The butcher's."

"Is the butcher in Turkey?"

They turned the corner before she answered.

I sat there thinking about the encounter. A young lad who thought he'd seen Father Christmas. A mother who knew he hadn't. I wouldn't normally give it a second thought.

And yet... The lad had been so insistent and the mother so determined to deny his story. Her denials had verged on the hostile. They were certainly evasive. A mum under pressure in the build-up to Christmas? Possibly. But I sensed there might be more to it than that.

I stood up and hurried after them in the direction of North Street. I spotted them crossing the road towards Hannington's.

Billy was still firing questions and Mum was shaking her head. The lad was an inquisitive little shaver. I could see him making a good journalist one day.

I hung back among the crowd of shoppers and followed. I was wondering how long it would take before they headed for home.

It takes me ten minutes to do my Christmas shopping. Well, you don't have the time to take longer at five twenty on Christmas Eve.

It took Billy's mum two and a quarter hours as she trailed around the shops. A butcher's, half a dozen newsagents and a tobacconist, and a greengrocer's. She didn't have much shopping at the end of it all. A turkey and a bag of chipolata sausages from the butcher's and the Brussels sprouts from the greengrocer's. What she'd been buying in those other shops was anybody's guess. But, then, she had one of those deep basket shopping bags and I couldn't see everything she'd put in it.

After she'd finished shopping, she tugged Billy towards the railway station. For a moment, I worried that they were going to catch a train, but she turned left and headed up Gloucester Road to the West Hill part of Brighton.

Billy and his Mum lived in a small terraced house just off Dyke Road. I watched her juggle her shopping as she fished in her handbag for a latchkey, unlock the door and push inside. I leaned on a lamppost at the other end of the street wondering what the hell I was doing.

I'd just traipsed after a middle-aged woman half way across Brighton on the strength of a hunch based on what? A feeling that I didn't like the woman? No, there was more to it than that. The way she'd reacted to Billy's Father Christmas story convinced me she was hiding something.

Billy mentioned that he'd seen Father Christmas in the garages at the back of the house. I waited a few moments, then made my way down the road.

An alley at the side of the terrace of houses led to a courtyard with eight garages at the back. There was a separate driveway in from the road which ran parallel with the back of the terrace. It was a miserable place, paved with oil-stained bricks and littered with rubbish – old petrol cans, rags, some broken windscreen wipers and other car parts I didn't recognise. There was a group of greasy dustbins up by a wall.

Nobody was about. I swiftly scanned the windows overlooking the courtyard. I took a moment to identify what must be Billy's bedroom. There was no little face pressed to the window pane.

I had a quick shufti round the garages. They were all locked. There were no signs that Father Christmas had been here. No strands of fur from Santa's robes. No skid marks from the sleigh. No reindeer droppings. Perhaps he was a phantom Father Christmas after all. A figment of Billy's imagination. Maybe I was wasting my time.

I walked towards the driveway that led through to the road and then I saw it - half hidden by a pile of dirty newspapers. A sack. Billy had said that he'd seen Father Christmas with his sack. I moved the newspapers to one side. The sack was brown, made out of hessian. The sort a gardener might buy from a hardware store to hold new season potatoes. There were no spuds in this one. It was clean, neatly folded and unused. But it looked as though it may have been hidden for use later.

I thought about that for a moment, then replaced the old newspapers. Billy had said he'd seen Father Christmas when he should have been in bed. I reckoned a lad of that age would probably be tucked up by eight o'clock. My guess was that he climbed out after his mum had read the bedtime story and kissed him goodnight. Then he'd spend a bit of time spying on the goings-on in the courtyard.

I decided that later in the evening I would join him.

It was ten past eight by the time I snuck up the alley beside the terrace.

I'd headed back to the office after my earlier visit. I'd wanted to check on who occupied the house. That meant consulting the electoral register held in the *Chronicle*'s newsroom. I'd discovered there was only one resident of voting age in the house – a Victoria Ann Meacher. I'd looked up the name in the *Chronicle*'s morgue, where all the press cuttings were kept. But there was nothing filed under that name.

I stepped cautiously into the garage courtyard, looked around for a place to hunker down out of sight. I spotted the dustbins I'd seen earlier and squeezed behind them. My shoe squelched as I trod in something soft. A smell of rotting greens overlain with curry sauce wafted up from the bins. If I had to stay for too long, I was going to find it difficult to move in decent company afterwards.

The courtyard was lit by a single lamp standard at the exit to the road. It threw a watery light across the bricked surface. The air was cold. I shivered.

I twisted round and looked up towards Billy's bedroom. The light was on, but as I watched it was switched off. I guessed Mum had said goodnight and had left her little darling to sleep.

I watched some more, expecting to see a pale face appear at the window or, at least, a twitch of the curtains. But Billy had either been ordered to stay in bed on pain of some terrible punishment or he was an expert in covert surveillance. Having seen the lad at close quarters, I suspected the latter.

After half an hour, I had acclimatised to the stink from the bins but my legs were doubled up and had less circulation than the *Church Times* at an atheists' convention. I shifted position to ease the pain and rattled one of the bins. I was fast concluding that I was wasting my time. Surely it would be easier to give Figgis his hundred fags? I decided to give it ten more minutes and head for the nearest pub.

Then headlights swung in from the road. A white Ford van turned a semi-circle through the courtyard and stopped outside the end garage in the block.

The driver's door opened and a small man dressed in a long red cloak trimmed with white fur climbed out. The hood of his cloak covered his head so that I couldn't see his face. But I could see that he had a long white beard. So Billy had seen Father Christmas.

The passenger door opened. A whippet-like man dressed in the red jerkin and green tights of an elf hurried round from the back. Santa's Little Helper.

Father Christmas crossed the courtyard, collected the sack from under the pile of newspapers and walked over to the garage. He pulled a large bunch of keys out of his pocket. He spent a few moments rattling through them until he found the right one, then opened the garage door. He disappeared inside.

A minute later he was outside with the sack on his back. This time, it was loaded with something heavy. The elf opened the back doors of the van and Father Christmas swung the sack inside. He shoved the doors shut and looked around.

I crouched lower behind the dustbins.

"That's the last of the French gaspers," he said. "Queenie has lined up some more buyers today."

"By royal appointment, then," the elf said.

The pair laughed, Father Christmas with a fine tenor ho, ho, ho, the elf with a high-pitched snigger.

"Yeah, French gaspers but English delivery," said Father Christmas.

"English delivery!" The elf was sniggering so much he was straining his tights and in danger of doing himself a serious injury.

"We'll drop these off, then head back to the flat for a bevvy," Father Christmas said.

They climbed into the van. The engine fired, the headlights sparked into life. And before I could crawl out from behind the dustbins, the van had vanished down the driveway and turned into the road.

I winced from the pain in my legs as the blood rushed back and stumbled against the dustbins. I thought about running after the van, but I'd never catch it. But I didn't need to. I still had plenty of questions, but the answers were closer to hand.

I hurried through the alleyway which led round to the front of Billy's Mum's house.

I was thinking hard.

It was Father Christmas who'd jolted my brain into action as violently as if he'd just plummeted down the chimney.

"French gaspers but English delivery," he'd said to his Little Helper. And the pair had laughed themselves silly.

165

He didn't mean English as in coming from England. He meant English as in belonging to Mr English.

I cursed myself for not remembering earlier. I'd heard a whisper that the police believed Frank English had been the robber behind the Newhaven bonded warehouse heist. He was a pint-sized Mr Big in Brighton's criminal underworld - with a vicious streak. Small and nasty, like a dung beetle. Trouble was, since the raid English had gone to ground. The police couldn't find him at any of his usual haunts.

But, then, they wouldn't have been looking for Father Christmas. And English had the kind of brass neck to try to fence his stolen fags before he left the area. Perhaps he needed the cash to disappear abroad. After all, he was looking at a capital charge. But English had a reputation for wriggling away from justice. I recalled covering a case at Lewes Assizes a couple of years earlier when English had been acquitted of armed robbery on alibi evidence.

And now I knew just why Billy's Mum was so insistent that the lad hadn't seen anything as he peered between his curtains searching for a glimpse of Father Christmas.

I reached the front of the house, stepped up to the door and knocked twice.

There was a moment's silence, then a rattling sound as a chain was put on. The door opened a couple of inches and an anxious face appeared.

"Mrs Victoria Meacher?" I asked.

She glanced nervously behind me. Saw the street was empty.

"Yes."

"Mrs Meacher, formerly Miss Victoria English."

166

"Who wants to know?"

I pulled out a card and handed it through the crack.

"Colin Crampton, *Evening Chronicle*. We met briefly in the Royal Pavilion gardens this morning."

"We don't want your type here." She started to push the door closed. I shoved my foot into the gap. Winced as she tried to ram the door shut.

"You can talk to me or the police," I said. "I can arrange them to be here in five minutes. What's it to be?"

"Don't bring the police here. Not with Billy in the house. Not just before Christmas."

"We can talk about that. Inside."

She thought about it for a moment, then rattled the chain out of its groove and opened the door.

She led me down a dimly lit narrow passage into the kitchen. There was a gas stove with some milk heating in a saucepan. She turned out the gas. Left the saucepan on the stove.

"For cocoa," she said. "Helps me sleep. I'll have it later."

There was a small deal table at the side of the kitchen with a couple of upright chairs. She motioned me towards one and we sat.

"Is Mr Meacher at home?"

She snorted. "Huh! The bastard walked out on me with a barmaid half his age seven years ago. Divorced him five years ago this Christmas."

"But you've kept your married name."

"So what?"

"You're Frank English's sister," I said. It was Victoria who'd given that perjured alibi evidence.

"Not a crime to be Frank's sister," she said.

"About the only thing in his life that hasn't been. I can understand why you wanted to hang on to your married name."

She snorted again.

"But you've been a very helpful little sister," I said.

"What do you mean?"

"You've been storing the haul from the Newhaven bonded warehouse heist in your garage."

"You think! There's nothing there."

"Not now, because over the last few nights Frank and his little helper have been moving it out."

"Frank's not been here. I don't know where he is."

"Perhaps not here. But I've just watched him take a sack of French cigarettes from the garage."

"Don't know anything about that."

"He was dressed as Father Christmas. Now I know why you were so anxious to deny that Billy had seen Santa. No doubt it was a clever idea on Frank's part to disguise himself. No-one is going to stop Father Christmas delivering a sack of toys for the kiddies. Except they weren't toys, were they?"

Victoria's thin lips were formed in a petulant pout. "Even if they weren't, I don't know where Frank's gone. I had nothing to do with it."

"I think you did. Because Frank said something else while I was hiding in the courtyard watching him and his little helper. He said, 'Queenie's lined up some more buyers today'. That's you – Queenie, a pet name for Victoria."

"I'm not the only Victoria in Brighton."

"True, but you're the only one who visited several newsagents and a tobacconist today while you were doing your Christmas shopping. I know, because I was watching you."

"Not a crime to go into a newsagent's. Besides, where I go is none of your business."

"I think it was Frank's business. I think you were touring the shops touting for orders for under-the-counter ciggies."

"Prove it."

"I don't have to. But I have made a mental note of the shops you called at. Wouldn't be too difficult for me to call at those shops and ask them whether they've got any special offers. I'm sure at least one will be indiscreet. The fags in the garage, the sales calls. Shouldn't be too difficult even for Brighton's finest to put together a case for handling stolen goods."

Victoria scowled at me. Looked at her milk. Thought about relighting the gas. Decided to leave it. Made up her mind about something.

"Frank made me do it – just as he forced me to give that evidence. I didn't want those damned cigarettes here. I told him."

"But you didn't have to help him sell the stuff."

Victoria laughed mirthlessly. "You don't argue with Frank. I found that out years ago."

"I need to know where Frank's hiding," I said.

"And you think I'm going to tell you? In your dreams."

"You fancy a spell inside yourself? They tell me prison can be a very lonely place at Christmas. Think you can handle it?"

"If I have to."

But the look on her face told me she wasn't sure.

A little voice said: "You're not going to prison. You're not, are you, Mum?"

We swung round. Billy was standing in the doorway. He was dressed in blue striped pyjamas. He had a threadbare dressing gown draped over his shoulders. He was clutching a stuffed panda with one ear.

And a single tear was rolling down his cheek.

Victoria's face crumpled.

Her lips quivered. Her hands were shaking. Her eyes glistened with unshed tears. Behind that defiant bluster was a worried mother. She started to mumble something, but I held up my hand to stop her.

I said: "Billy, your Mum's not going to prison. I'm going to help her – because she's going to help me."

I stared hard at her. "That is right, isn't it?" I said.

She held my look for what seemed like a minute. Then she gave one short, reluctant nod.

She crossed to Billy. Put her arms around him. Gave him a tight hug. "Mummy's not going to prison, darling," she said. "Now go back to bed. Tomorrow's Christmas Eve. I'm taking you to see Father Christmas at Hannington's."

"The same Father Christmas I've seen out the back window?" Billy asked.

"No," she said. "The real one."

"It's been a good many years since we've had such a strong front page splash on Christmas Eve," said Frank Figgis.

We were in his office. It was late afternoon on Christmas Eve. Figgis was lounging back in his chair with his feet on the desk. I could see the Christmas lights in North Road from his window. I could hear the faint strains of the Sally Army band outside the Chapel Royal. They were playing *God Rest ye Merry, Gentlemen*.

I decided after delivering Figgis his Christmas story, I deserved a little merriment. I picked up the night final edition and looked again at the headline:

FATHER CHRISTMAS ARRESTED IN DAWN RAID

"Clever ploy by Frank English disguising himself as Santa," said Figgis.

"It was the only way he could move around Brighton without being recognised," I said. "He had to retrieve what he'd stolen and fence them before the police caught up with him."

"What I can't understand is how you discovered where he was hiding out."

"I had a little help there," I said.

"And it was a bit of luck that he was still wearing the Santa get-up when the police burst in."

"Word has it he was too drunk to take it off," I said.

Figgis heaved his feet off the desk and leaned forward. "Suppose you've delivered on the Christmas story," he said.

"Suppose I have."

I stood up and moved towards the door.

"Still not everyone in the newsroom managed it," he said. He reached out and patted the large pile of cigarette packets on his desk. "No need to guess what I'm getting for Christmas."

I turned at the door. "Lung cancer?" I said. "Merry Christmas."

Peter Bartram

Peter Bartram brings years of experience as a journalist to his Crampton of the Chronicle crime mysteries. Peter began his career during a "gap year" between school and university when he worked as a reporter for the Worthing Herald. After graduating from the London School of Economics, Peter resumed his life as a journalist working for newspapers and magazines in London.

Peter has done most things in journalism – from door-stepping for quotes to writing serious editorials. He's covered stories in locations as different as 700-feet down a coal mine and Buckingham Palace. He's edited newspapers and magazines and written 20 non-fiction books.

There are currently 11 books in the Crampton series with well over 100,000 readers around the world. Crime book reviewers have praised the books as "fast paced", "superbly crafted", "a breath of fresh air", and "a romp of a read". Ordinary readers had awarded the books well over 600 five-star reviews at the last count.

Peter Bartram is a Chindi Author.

Chindi Authors

Chindi, a network of authors based mainly in Sussex, was formed in 2014 so that local independent authors could support and encourage each other. Recently Chindi has been exploring wider horizons. While some members have gained traditional publishing contracts, others prefer the autonomy of indie publishing.

Chindi organises events, such as popular ghost tours of Littlehampton and Chichester, and runs workshops and panels for writers at Sussex arts festivals. In its role as publisher, Chindi has produced two anthologies – 'Littlehampton Ghost Tour' and the forthcoming 'A Feast of Christmas Stories' – and co-published a second ghost tour book for Chichester.

Members meet regularly, both in person and through internet conferencing, to share ideas and suggest projects. One of these projects is Chindi Speaks: a group of 14 writers who speak on subjects as diverse as romantic and historical fiction, humour, children's literature, history and self-help. Our YouTube channel offers a taster.

The membership is capped at 40 and aspiring Chindi authors are expected to demonstrate a professional standard of work. To learn more about Chindi, meet its authors, sample their books or apply to join, go to www.chindi-authors.co.uk. The Chindi Speaks booklet is available on request from Rosemary Noble at chirosie272@googlemail.com

Aldwick Publishing

If you have enjoyed this book you may also be interested in:

Meet The Winners, the 2019 West Sussex & Hampshire finalists in the Bognor Regis Write Club's first short story competition;

A Blast On The Waverley's Whistle, Bognor Regis Write Club's 1st Anthology;

The View From Here, Bognor Regis Write Club's 2nd Anthology;

News of Leon & Other Tales, a collection of short stories, written by Julia Macfarlane;

Chichester Ghost Tour, a self-guided walk around the city centre, also available as a guided tour by private arrangement with Julia Macfarlane (bognorwriters@gmail.com) – a great way to raise funds for charity or for a social event.

All books available on Amazon, in local bookshops or from:

Aldwick Publishing (info@aldwickpublishing.com).

Aldwick Publishing also has other books you may be interested in. Why not take a look at Bruce Macfarlane's **Time Travel Diaries** series at **www.aldwickpublishing.com**?

Best Selling Romantic Comedies, set in West Sussex!

 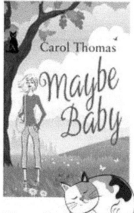

The Lisa Blake series

★★★★★

"A wonderful story, with charming characters and adorable pets."

"Fun, romantic, and heartwarming; filled with friendship and love."

 Published by Ruby Fiction
www.carol-thomas.co.uk

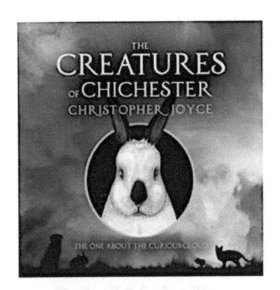

Also by Christopher Joyce
www.creaturesofchichester.com

DO YOUR KIDS LOVE WRITING?

Why not join our free #kidsclub?

For more information visit:

www.lexirees.co.uk

 @LexiAuthor

 @lexi_rees

*Life, love and laughter
in the land of sun and vines*

At Home in the Pays d'Oc

Tales from the Pays d'Oc

The Pays d'Oc series

Patricia Feinberg Stoner

www.paw-prints-in-the-butter.com

One Stop
Fiction
★ ★ ★ ★ ★
Book Award

Lightning Source UK Ltd.
Milton Keynes UK
UKHW041809131019
351541UK00001B/20/P